P9-DIH-503

the
fat girl

Marilyn Sachs

the fat girl

Woodbury, Minnesota

Second Edition
Third Printing, 2009
(Formerly titled *The Fat Girl*, published by Dutton Children's Books, 1984)

Book design by Steffani Sawyer
Cover design by Lisa Novak
Cover photograph © 2006 Nathanial Young/Acclaim Images

Flux, an imprint of Llewellyn Publications

The Cataloging-in-Publication Data for *The Fat Girl* is on file at the Library of Congress.

ISBN 13: 978-0-7387-1000-6
ISBN 10: 0-7387-1000-8

Flux
A Division of Llewellyn Worldwide, Ltd.
2143 Wooddale Drive, Dept. 978-0-7387-1000-6
Woodbury, MN 55125-2989, U.S.A.
www.fluxnow.com

Printed in the United States of America

For Zoe Borkowski,
good and indispensable friend

one

The only way I could get out of Mr. Wasserman's chemistry class was to register for something else at the same time. There weren't many choices.

"Since when have you been interested in ceramics?" my advisor asked, his nose twitching suspiciously.

"Oh, I've always been interested in ceramics," I told him, trying to get the right look of honest enthusiasm into my face.

"Come on, Lyons," he said, "get off it. Guys like you give me a pain! You're only trying to get out of Mr. Wasserman's class. You can't fool me."

"Uh uh," I said earnestly, shaking my head. "I really

want to take that ceramics class. I've been wanting to take that class ever since I started high school, but I never could fit it in."

"Well, you can't fit it in now either. It conflicts with your chemistry class."

"There is another chemistry class," I reminded him gently, "in the fourth period."

"It's filled," he said.

"Well, I did go over and talk to Mrs. Humphreys just before I came here, and she said if it was all right with you, she could squeeze me in."

My advisor looked at me with disgust. Behind me, at least ten other students waited to see him, and a low, restless growl permeated his small office. He was pressured and I knew it, and he knew I knew it. "You're just handing me a line of bull," he said. "None of you kids want to work. That's the trouble. That's the way it is with all of you. But I'll tell you something, Lyons. If you're planning to go to college, you'll learn a lot more about chemistry in Mr. Wasserman's class."

As usual, my advisor was missing the point completely. I did want to go to college, and that was why I couldn't afford to take Mr. Wasserman's course. I already had a couple of Cs and didn't need another one. Everybody knew that Wasserman was a tough marker, so I wasn't taking any chances.

"I really want to take ceramics," I told him. "I've always wanted to take ceramics."

Later, on the way to the ceramics class, I figured I would wait a couple of weeks before dropping it. My advisor wasn't particularly vindictive, but he might've just switched me back into Wasserman's class if I had irritated him too much.

I never did drop ceramics that term. Instead, I fell in love and spent the best and the most miserable year of my life. All because Mr. Wasserman was such a hard marker. None of any of this would have happened if it wasn't for him.

The fat girl and I arrived at the door at the same time. Since she was twice my width, it was obvious that we couldn't get through the door at the same time. So I gallantly stood back and held out my arm, directing her to go first. Somebody behind me snickered, and she looked up at me as if I'd goosed her.

"I didn't do anything," I said.

She hurried inside and I turned, raising my eyebrows at the guy in back of me. "What a butt!" he said. "Did you ever see anything like that before?"

Inside, people were already working. You have to understand that ceramics is a religion to its disciples. They don't do anything else but worship clay. They eat, sleep, drink pots. Nothing else matters. Some of the people in the class had been taking ceramics for years. They came before classes started in the morning and during their lunch hours, and they stayed as long as they could into the afternoon until Ms. Holland, the teacher, threw them out.

She wasn't in sight when we first arrived. The fat girl moved off to a corner, and the rest of us newcomers stood around at the front of the room, waiting and watching the regulars. At the back of the room, a girl was slamming clay down on a table. She threw it down, picked it up, and slammed it down again. A few kids were sitting at a long table, working on various clay projects, their faces solemn and intent. At one side of the room, two others were turning pots on potter's wheels. Then somebody cried out, "Oh, my God, how gorgeous!"

A girl came through the door at the back, from the kiln room, holding up a large, round bowl. She was caressing the bowl, running one hand up and down its side in a way that made me feel warm.

"Look at this," she hollered. "I added a little copper

oxide and just look at that color. It's so beautiful I can't stand it."

A few people stopped their work to murmur approval. The guy next to me, in a low voice, made an unflattering comment about what he thought the pot could've been used for. But I hardly listened because I had fallen in love.

The girl looked like what I had been dreaming about ever since I started dreaming about girls. She was tall and slim and very fair, with long blonde hair flowing down her shoulders and deep, deep blue eyes.

I cleared my throat. "It's beautiful," I said. "How did you do it?"

"Well, I mixed copper oxide with my standard mottled semigloss glaze and . . ." she began, moving over toward me and speaking in an excited voice. Close up, I noticed a tiny ridge of pimples between her eyes and also that her ears were rather large and stuck out. But aside from that, she was about as perfect as a girl could be.

Her name was Norma Jenkins. She sat next to me once the class started and gave me a lot of useful information about clay. I didn't hear any of it. I was busy admiring her even, white teeth and blessing Mr. Wasserman.

On Friday, I helped her carry four pots home from school.

"Don't you do anything else?" I asked her. "I mean besides make pots?"

"Sure I do," she said, "lots of things."

"Like what?"

"Well, I . . . I . . . No." She began laughing. "Not too much. I've had a love affair with clay since I was eight, I guess."

"Only clay?" I said, my elbow brushing against hers.

"Be careful," she cried, holding out her arm. "That pitcher . . . I'm going to give it to my mother for her birthday."

There was a clay smudge on her chin and her fingernails were caked with a pale, green glaze. Around us, a cold San Francisco fog pressed down against our heads. I remember looking at her pink cheeks, at the alarm in her face over the thought I might break her pitcher, and I felt warm and happy to be alive.

"Only clay?" I repeated, cradling the pitcher against my chest.

"What?"

"I mean, you've had a love affair only with clay? Nothing . . . nobody else?"

Her cheeks grew even pinker. "Well, there was this boy . . . he took ceramics last year . . . he made some nice mugs but . . ." She shook her head. "He really didn't understand glazes."

"Is that why you broke up with him?"

"No . . . Anyway, he broke up with me."

"Because you knew more about glazes?"

"Now you're laughing at me." She tilted her head and laughed up at me. I was so happy, I pressed the pitcher hard against my chest and heard her shriek, "Watch out, you'll break it!"

"So why did he break up with you?"

"Because he found somebody he liked better," she said carefully.

"The jerk!"

"No," she said softly, "he wasn't. I mean, he isn't a jerk. He's very nice, very smart, but I guess he just found somebody he liked better. I guess she's a nice girl. She's more interested in the kinds of things he likes to do. I don't know her—she never took ceramics—but I guess she's nice."

I snorted.

"I felt bad for a while, but I'm over it now."

"I'm glad," I told her, and we both smiled quickly at each other and looked away.

"How about you?" she asked. Our elbows brushed again, but this time she didn't yell anything about her pot.

"Oh, I went around with a girl in my sophomore year. She was the big one in my life. Then there were a few in between, and this summer there was somebody I met at the hardware store—I work part-time at a hardware store—but she was kind of a birdbrain, talked on the phone all the time, and had a weird laugh. That's all over now."

"How about the girl in your sophomore year?"

"Kendra Gin?"

"Kendra Gin? I know her. She's gorgeous."

"Yeah, I guess she is."

"Was the girl this summer . . . was she pretty too?"

"Yeah, I guess she was."

"I guess you like pretty girls."

"I guess everybody likes pretty girls."

"Well," she said, very seriously, "it doesn't matter to me. I mean, I don't care whether a guy is good-looking or not. It's what's inside that counts."

"Sure," I told her, "that's important too, but I don't think I'd ever be attracted to a girl who wasn't pretty. I mean, she has to be pretty for me to get interested in her, and then, after that, there has to be something inside for me to stay interested."

She argued with me. She said that physical beauty was only skin-deep. She said to look only for physical beauty was superficial and demeaning. Her voice was husky and filled with warmth. We walked together through the gray fog, arguing—comfortable and happy in the certain knowledge that both of us were good-looking, and that something powerful was beginning between us.

two

I didn't tell my mother about Norma for a couple of weeks. Not that she wouldn't have been interested. She was interested in everything I did and in everybody I liked. She was always asking me to tell her what was happening in my life, but whatever I told her, it was never right. Most of the time I didn't tell her anything. But that wasn't right, either.

"So how was school today, Jeff?"

"Okay, Mom."

"Anything unusual happen?"

"Nope."

"How are your marks?"

"Pretty good, I guess."

"Whatever happened to that friend of yours you used to be so close to last year? What's his name?"

"Jim?"

"No, the other one—short boy with very good manners. I liked him."

"Fred? Oh—Fred Waller. He moved, Mom. His family moved away to Chicago."

"You never told me."

"Mom, it's six months at least."

"Well, you never said anything. You never tell me anything."

I don't like to tell her anything because she always feels bad when I do. Like when she found out about Norma.

"Who is Norma, Jeff?"

"She's in my ceramics class, Mom."

"Well, she calls you an awful lot. Wanda says you're on the phone with her all the time."

"Wanda's got a big mouth."

"And I know you've been spending a lot of time over at her house. You're never home weekends anymore." My mother was smiling now. "You can tell me, Jeff. I'll keep your secret."

"Well . . ." I looked over at her. The two of us were

sitting together at the kitchen table after dinner. My sister, Wanda, was out of the room, probably taking another shower.

"Well . . ." I started laughing and my mother laughed too. She's a little woman with a thin, dark, worried face. She doesn't smile too often. Maybe she used to before my father left her, but it was so many years ago I can't really remember. Anyway, I get this happy feeling when she laughs. It catches me off guard, makes me forget that it never lasts.

"Another notch in your belt, Jeff?"

"Oh no, Mom. Norma's different. All those others were just pretty faces. She . . ."

"Doesn't have a pretty face?" My mother was still laughing. She reached over and patted my hand.

"Oh, she's gorgeous, Mom, but she's really a special person, a wonderful person."

"So when do I meet her?"

"Well . . ."

"Why don't you invite her over to dinner this weekend? You're always over at her house. You eat there all the time. Her mother must be a great cook."

"No, she's a lousy cook, Mom. Not like you."

My mother has two little dimples in her face when

she smiles. I don't see them very often, and I watched them as I went on.

"She's a lousy cook, but she likes to can things. Her kids complain because she's got like hundreds of jars down in the basement—things like quince jam and pickles and figs. She keeps telling me to take some, but . . ."

"I like quince jam," said my mother, still smiling. But suddenly there was a little edge there, like she was thinking why didn't I think of her? Why didn't I remember she liked quince jam and bring her a lousy jar?

"Her kids complain all the time," I hurried on, "but she keeps right on canning things."

"What does she do," said my mother, still pleasant, "when she's not canning?"

"Oh, she doesn't work. Norma says she's one of the few women left in the world who doesn't feel guilty about being a housewife."

"Just stays at home," my mother murmured, and picked up a few crumbs on the table with one hand and dropped them into her other hand.

"Well, she doesn't really have to work. They're loaded. Mr. Jenkins is a lawyer, and they live in a big house on Jackson Street. It's a great house, but it's kind of a mess because Mrs. Jenkins isn't much of a housekeeper. All she does is can stuff and listen to opera records."

My mother's face relaxed. I should have stopped, but I didn't. That's the trouble. Once I start, I never know when to stop.

"But she's gorgeous, Mom. They're all gorgeous in that family. Norma says she's the ugly duckling, and I guess she's right. Because as beautiful as she is, her two sisters are even more beautiful. And her mother—her mother's a real knockout. Even though she must be around forty, she's got to be the most beautiful woman I ever . . ."

My mother stood up, her little dark face tight again. "Sure she's gorgeous," said my mother. "All she's got to do is sit around her big house and do nothing. What's she got to worry about with a rich husband and more money than she knows what to do with?"

"The house is a mess," I cried desperately, but it was too late.

"No wonder you're never home anymore," said my mother, that tight, sharp edge twisting in her voice. "I guess you like mingling with the beautiful people."

My mother turned her back to me and started washing the dishes. I tried to remember exactly what I had said that changed everything this time.

“What did I say?” I said. “What are you all worked up over?”

She turned off the water and twisted around to face me. “Nothing,” she said. “You didn’t say anything. You never tell me anything. I have to pull it out of you.”

“But anything I tell you, you get upset. Even if you just ask me the time and I tell you, you get upset.”

“Because you’re selfish,” she said, not shouting, never shouting. When my mother gets angry, her voice sinks lower and lower and comes out between her teeth. “All you think about is going off with your rich friends and forgetting you have a mother and sister. I’m working forty hours a week, and I don’t have the time to sit around listening to opera and looking beautiful.”

“Mom, Mom . . .”

“And all I ask is for you to help just a little . . . pick up a few things at the store, run the washing machine once in a while, check up on Wanda. But you only think of yourself . . . just like your father.”

Then I was shouting. I always ended up shouting, and banging my chair into the table, and storming off into my room and slamming the door.

Just like my father! Sooner or later, when she really wants to insult me, she says I’m just like my father. She knows it will hurt me, even though I never understand exactly why it does. When we were little, Wanda and I used to wait for him to come home from work, because that was when the good times started, when my father came home from work.

After he left, he always said we could come and stay with him whenever we wanted. He doesn't live far away, but now the good times belong to his new wife, Linda, and his new little kids, Sean and David. They're cute kids, and they wait for my father now, their father too, and whoop it up and jump all over him when he comes home. I don't go over there very much anymore.

My mother is a nurse. She works at San Francisco General Hospital five days a week and then spends the rest of her time cleaning our apartment and cooking fantastic meals for the three of us. Nobody can cook like my mother. If I ever eat a meal at a friend's house and tell her how good it was, she'll always cook the same thing for me at home, only better.

Norma came for dinner the next weekend. My mother had set the dining room table with a white cloth, and you could still smell the silver polish on the candlesticks, which hadn't been used since last Christmas. Norma brought a jar of quince jam and two jars of tomato chutney.

"I hope you like it, Mrs. Lyons," Norma said. "We keep begging my mother to stop, but she won't."

"Please thank your mother very much," said my mother formally. She was dressed up in high heels and a green silk dress.

Norma was wearing jeans and an Indian blouse. Her idea of dressing up was washing her face and combing her hair. As ever, there was a distinct line of dark clay and glaze under her fingernails.

My mother's eyes kept returning to those fingernails whenever Norma reached for something on the table, which was often.

"I never tasted homemade rolls before," said Norma, taking a third. "These are marvelous."

"They're a little heavy, I think," said my mother.

"What a wonderful soup!" Norma said, accepting a second bowl. "My mother once made *avgolemono*, but it didn't taste anything like this."

"It's too watery, and I don't think I used enough lemon," from my mother.

Norma managed to eat all her chicken and walnuts and have doubles on my mother's apple torte. "You must be the best cook I've ever met," she told my mother, her cheeks even pinker than usual from all the exertion of eating and her blue eyes bulging. "You could win a prize with that apple torte."

"The apples were too mushy," said my mother.

Norma offered to help with the dishes, but my mother refused. She said Wanda would help.

"It's not my turn," Wanda said.

"All right, I'll do it myself," said my mother in her suffering voice.

"I'd really like to help," said Norma. "I do them more than anybody else in my house, except maybe my father. The others don't mind how many days they pile up in the sink, but the two of us can't stand the smell. My mother even forgets to turn on the dishwasher."

My mother gave her a pitying smile. "It's all right," she said. "I don't have any special plans for tonight, so why don't the three of you just run along and enjoy yourselves."

"I'll help," Wanda said in a sulky voice. She's fourteen and looks and sounds a lot like my mother.

"They're real nice," Norma said when we were sitting in my room, "your mother and your sister."

"It's all right, Norma," I told her. "You don't have to say it."

"No, I mean it." Norma's head was resting on my

shoulder. I kissed her hair and smelled the slightly sour clay smell that never left her.

"And she's a marvelous cook."

"I told you she was," I said, stroking her warm arm.

"And your little sister's cute. She looks a lot like your mother. They're both dark and small. But who do you look like?"

"My father."

"Do you have a picture of him?"

I opened the dictionary on my desk to *O* and pulled out one of the pictures I had of my father. It was taken when I was about five, a couple years before he left. The two of us were standing on the beach, both wearing blue trunks and both grinning at each other.

"He looks just like you," she said. "But why do you keep this picture in the dictionary?"

"Because I don't want my mother to feel bad."

"Why would she feel bad? He's still your father, isn't he?"

I put the picture back in the dictionary and sat down on my bed again. But it was hard to concentrate on Norma. Neither of us could relax the way we could at her house.

three

The first time I noticed the fat girl watching me was while I was rolling out some clay for a slab plate I was planning to make. I just looked up suddenly and caught her staring at me, her little eyes deep, deep inside all that fat in her face. She looked away, and I checked my fly and went back to my clay.

But after that, it happened all the time. I'd be working away and suddenly I could sense her huge shape, off to one side or sometimes even behind me, motionless, watching.

"Why is the fat girl watching me all the time?" I complained to Norma. "She even watches what I'm making.

The other day I caught her looking at my tiles on the drying rack."

Norma was turning a deep, narrow vase on the potter's wheel, and I stood next to her. She murmured something, but all her attention was focused on the spinning shape before her. I watched her hands join with the clay, shaping it and pulling it up and out. Her body moved rhythmically back and forth as the wheel turned, almost as if she were praying.

There were three great potters in the class—Norma, Roger Torres, and Dolores Kabotie. Ms. Holland joked around with them as if they were her friends and let them come in to work on their own projects whenever they liked. In exchange, they helped her load and unload the kiln, worked with the beginning students, and generally supervised the shop when she wasn't around. They were the inner circle.

"I guess I've been studying the longest, ever since I was eight," Norma told me. "But Roger took classes with Ida O'Neill, the best potter in the city, and Dolores says her grandfather was a famous Indian potter."

"But we know who really is the best, don't we?" I said.

"No, Jeff, really . . ."

"Come on, Norma, you know you're the best."

Norma's cheeks turned pink, but she shook her head. "I can throw pretty well on the wheel, maybe better than the others. But Dolores makes most of her pots by the coil method anyway, like the Indians do, and her shapes are wonderful. Her designs are better than mine too. And Roger's glazes—especially his blues and greens . . ."

"Well, I'm an impartial observer, Norma. And when it comes to shapes, nobody's can come up to yours."

I was happy with Norma, but I was jealous too. Jealous, to begin with, because she was so tied up with her pots and so good at it. And then I was jealous of all the attention she was always getting from other guys. When a girl's a beauty like Norma and like all the girls I ever liked, you know every other guy's going to be after her. I hated it with my old girlfriends, and I hated it with Norma. I'd wait for her in the hall sometimes and watch her come along, admiring that quick, bounding step she had, her long, blonde hair spraying out behind her shining face. You could see guys watching her, calling out to her, smiling at her. I hated it, even though Norma didn't play games like so many of the other girls I'd gone out with. She didn't flirt, I knew that, and I knew I didn't have to worry about her, but I still hated it.

She taught me to throw on the wheel, how to center the wobbling clay, and how to begin to shape it.

"That's it, a little more water! Brace your elbow against your body! Fine! Fine! Now get your left hand around the clay. Keep the wheel going. Get your right hand ready to open it up. That's right! That's right! That's *right!*"

I caught her passion and started coming into the classroom on my lunch hour, and sometimes I even stayed after school with the inner circle. In their presence, I was humble. I watched as magnificent shapes rose up under their hands, and I cursed and fumed as my own clumsy, thick-walled pots never seemed to improve in beauty.

"Patience, patience!" Norma urged. "Rome wasn't built in a day. You're doing very well—much, much better than most of the beginners. Just look at Ellen De Luca's pots."

"Who?"

"Ellen De Luca."

"Oh, the fat girl. Thanks a lot for comparing me to her."

The fat girl couldn't do anything right. Not only was she fat, but she was clumsy as well. She was always slamming doors, bumping into people, and dropping things. Any time you'd hear a crack, you could be sure the fat girl had broken something, and you could only hope it wasn't something that belonged to you, like the time she knocked my teapot off the drying shelf.

"Oh, Jeff, I'm sorry!"

"Sorry!" I yelled as I picked up the pieces and cradled them against me. "Sorry!"

"I know it was such a beautiful teapot. I was being so careful."

"It was beautiful," I snarled. "Damn it! It was the best thing I've done so far. Damn it! Damn it!"

Well, maybe it was the best thing I'd done so far, if you like heavy, clumsy pots with pug-nosed spouts. I'd never really appreciated it as much as when I saw it in pieces on the ground.

"I'm sorry. I wish I could do something."

I looked at her in disgust. She was wearing one of those pale-blue-polyester-pants-and-matching-short-sleeve-blouse outfits that middle-aged women wear, and her huge arms came billowing out of the sleeves. Her features seemed very small in her fat face, and her muddy-colored hair hung limp on her head. What a sight!

"I'm really sorry, Jeff. I wish I could make it up to you."

And how did she know my name? I could never remember hers. And why did she keep watching me? And what right did she have to admire my pots anyway?

"Look," I said, "do me a favor. Just keep away from my things. Okay?"

"Okay," she said. She had a very tiny, squeaky voice, which seemed bizarre coming from such a hulk.

"Okay," she said, nodding and smiling a kind of pleading, frightened smile that made me want to punch her. I moved away as fast as I could.

Norma worked with her. Before you could begin throwing on the wheel, you were supposed to make a slab tile, a pinch bowl, and also a bowl made by the coil method. The fat girl managed to turn out a lumpy tile and a clumsy, lopsided pinch bowl, but she couldn't seem to get the hang of coils. Norma worked with her patiently. You could hear how she slowed her voice down, as if the fat girl were a retarded eight-year-old.

"Now just don't push so hard when you're rolling the coils. No, no, keep them even! Try not to let them lump up in the middle. No, you're leaning too hard! Just roll them lightly. No, no . . ."

Her coils bulged, and so did her pot.

"It looks like her," I told Norma.

"Shh! Shh! She'll hear you. Stop it!"

The fat girl caught me kissing Norma in the kiln room one day. Another time, she was watching while I ran an appreciative hand down Norma's back as she bent over to dip one of her pots in the glaze bucket. Any time I'd look in her direction, she'd quickly look away, so I knew she was spying on me. I didn't know why, and I hated it.

"I'm just going to tell her off one of these days," I told Norma.

"Forget it, Jeff. Leave her alone, poor thing. She can't help it."

"Can't help weighing over two hundred pounds? The slob. Why doesn't she just stop eating? She's disgusting."

"Maybe it's a medical problem," Norma said. "Don't be so hard on her."

"I'm not hard on her. I just want her to leave me alone."

But Norma was brushing leaf patterns on some large square plates she was planning to give her family for Christmas, and she didn't answer.

Norma's house was filled with bowls and vases and mugs and pitchers and teapots and urns. It was a wonderful, messy house where none of the rooms seemed to have limits. In my house, each room had a distinct function and purpose. The kitchen was for cooking, the dining room for eating, the bedrooms for sleeping. But in Norma's house, all activities spilled from one room into another. Even though most of the cooking took place in the kitchen, Mrs. Jenkins had her stereo there too, so she could listen to her opera records while she worked. All of the kids did their homework in the kitchen, and books, papers, and pencils mingled with the pots and pans. The living room looked like the dining room, and the dining room table was generally too crowded with Norma's pots to allow anybody to eat there without a great effort. None of the children ever seemed to stay in his or her own bedroom.

"Carmen wanders around at night and usually ends up sleeping on the couch. And Joey usually sleeps either in Lucia's room or mine. He's afraid of vampires and can't sleep by himself," Norma told me.

Joey was the youngest, seven years old, and the only boy. There were two sisters between him and Norma—Carmen, who was fifteen, and Lucia, who was twelve.

"Your mother should try to make him sleep in his own room," I said.

"Why?"

"Because he's got to get over it."

"Why?"

"Well—kids will make fun of him. He's a boy, and he doesn't want to be a sissy."

Norma was looking at me and smiling. There was a sore, jealous place in my stomach. "I used to be afraid of the dark," I told her.

"And?"

"My mother—she made me get over it." It was a long time ago, but I could still remember her voice outside the closed door, saying over and over again, "Stay in your room, Jeff. There's nothing to be afraid of." And me, pleading, "Just don't lock it, and I'll stay inside. Please, Mom, don't lock the door."

"How?"

"She put a lock on the outside of the door to stop me from coming out and waking her up."

Norma stopped smiling. She patted my hand. "Poor Jeff," she said.

"No, no!" I protested. "She never used it. She just showed me it was there, and it worked. Honestly, Norma, she's not like that. I did get over it, and I'm not afraid anymore."

"Everybody's afraid of something," Norma said. "It's not so terrible to be afraid."

Sometimes the noise in Norma's house was deafening. Arguments could start in an upstairs bathroom, crackle down the stairs into the living room, explode in the dining room, and echo all through the house. There would be Mrs. Jenkins' opera stars screeching away in the kitchen, Mr. Jenkins' TV set going full blast in the upstairs den, Joey's cars and trucks hurtling through the house, while Carmen, who took ballet lessons and looked like a pale green-gold water goddess, danced in all of the rooms.

"My mother named each of us for an opera," Norma said, making a face. "I mean each of us girls. I think I got off easy."

"How about Joey? Who is he named for?"

"Joe DiMaggio."

"Is that an opera?"

"Come on, Jeff. You know Joe DiMaggio was a famous ballplayer for the Yankees. My father's crazy about baseball. My mother wanted to call him Giovanni after Mozart's opera, but my father insisted on Joe."

I loved Norma's house, loved being lost in the litter that overflowed everywhere. My own house was so neat and orderly, a person always stood out. Here, I never felt the spotlight on me—I blended into the clutter. Sometimes my own training was too much for me though, and I found myself straightening crooked pictures on the wall, hanging up Norma's jacket when she flung it on the floor, and mopping up ancient milk spills under the kitchen table.

It wasn't always easy to find a quiet, private place in Norma's house. And often it was fun being with the others, listening to Norma's old Maria Callas records, looking over Mr. Jenkins' historic collection of baseball cards, or playing Dungeons & Dragons with Lucia and her friends.

But the best times were with Norma. We'd climb upstairs to her messy room filled with years of pots, and turn out the cat or the dog or Joey, and sit down on her unmade bed and hold each other and kiss and touch and be in love. We never went all the way. What was the hurry? I knew there were going to be years and years of love between Norma and me. And there would have been. If it hadn't been for the fat girl.

four

Her name was Ellen De Luca. But I never thought of her with a name until the day I made her cry.

"She's gross," I told Norma. "She was in the cafeteria yesterday, sitting at the next table. She wolfed down two cheeseburgers and then must have eaten about six candy bars. She threw the wrappers under the table too, so she's a litterbug as well as a disgusting slob."

Norma made a face. "Will you get off it?" she said. "You go on and on about her."

"Because she's a real pain. She watches me all the time."

"But Jeff, you're watching her too."

She was right. I was watching her. Not only in the ceramics class, but everywhere else too. I'd see her waddling along in the hall, the loose flesh on her arms jiggling as she walked. I always looked away, avoiding her eyes. I never said hello. Most people looked away when they saw her, the way you do when anybody deformed is in sight. She generally kept her eyes down too and walked by herself. Sometimes a kid would talk to her in that loud, hearty voice you keep for the handicapped to show them that it doesn't make any difference to you.

But it does.

"I don't understand how she ever could have allowed herself to get that way. I mean, she must be about seventeen, and she looks like an old woman."

Norma was stuffing paper into a pair of Adidas. We were going to a Halloween costume party at Roger Torres' house, and she was wearing my clothes. She had on my T-shirt with a picture of Burt Reynolds that said BURT REYNOLDS IS ONLY A 10. I'M A 15. It flopped all over her, and so did my jeans. But nothing could ever stop her from looking beautiful.

She managed to fit her feet into my Adidas, tied the laces, stood up, and giggled when she looked at me.

I wanted to go to the party wearing her clothes, but

since all she ever wore were jeans and old shirts, we both decided it wouldn't be funny. So here I was, wriggling around in an old pink tutu of Carmen's and wearing a lot of lipstick and makeup.

"You better keep away from Castro Street," she said. "You really do look bee-yoo-ti-ful."

We twined our arms around each other and stood in front of the mirror, inspecting ourselves. The funny thing was—I did look beautiful. Tall and big as I am, and wearing the ridiculous tutu, I looked good enough to almost turn myself on.

"You know something?" Norma said.

"What?"

"We're lucky."

I knew what she meant, but I asked "Why?" anyway.

"Because we never have to worry about looking good. So many things you have to worry about in life, but that's one thing we'll never have to worry about."

"You can never tell," I said, watching in the mirror as I bent down to kiss the top of Norma's head. "Maybe I'll get bald and have hair sprouting out of my nose, and maybe you'll lose your teeth and get fat like the fat girl."

"Poor thing," said Norma.

"The slob!" I said.

Lots of the kids from the ceramics class were at the party, but not the fat girl.

"How come you didn't invite the fat girl?" I asked Roger.

"I didn't know you had a thing for her," he said. Roger was a short, dark, very muscular guy. He was planning to become a ceramic designer and work on developing new glazes. He and Dolores Kabotie had been going around together for a long time, and both of them were dressed up as figures from a Grecian urn. Dolores was dressed in a long, white dress, but Roger was only wearing a skimpy pair of shorts.

"He's always got to be showing off his rippling muscles," I muttered to Norma. Roger took weight lifting classes and was proud of his bod.

"Actually, the men wear a lot less than that on the Grecian urns."

"Too bad the women don't," I said. "It's not fair that Dolores has to be all covered up."

"Well, she is a little thick in the thigh, and her bust is kind of droopy."

"Meow!" I said. "You know, Norma, sometimes I think you're jealous of Dolores."

"Me—jealous of Dolores?" We both looked over at

the dark, intense girl whose dumpy figure was encased in white. Roger was pretending to be playing a panpipe and dancing around her.

"She's actually not bad looking."

"She has a very nice face," Norma said kindly, with the generosity of one who knew she was much more beautiful. "And if she lost a little weight . . ." Norma sighed. "I guess I am jealous. The three of us are too close. It's practically incestuous. We've been working together for years and trying to act like we're not competing with each other. But did you see that stunning pot she finished yesterday, with the wide bottom and narrow top and those geometric designs? I could never do anything like that—never!"

Roger moved over toward me, still playing his panpipes, and the kids started shouting for me to get up and dance. So up I rose, flung my arms up in the air, balanced on the tippy toes of my basketball sneakers, and twirled around, stepping on as many feet as I could and landing finally in Norma's arms. She laughed so hard, she forgot all about being jealous of Dolores Kabotie.

But not me. I was jealous of Dolores Kabotie, and I was jealous of Roger Torres and of Norma too. I was jealous of all three of them. Because they were set—they knew what they were going to do with their lives. All of them were going into ceramics—Roger as a designer, and the two girls as professional potters. And they were good. Nobody came up to them in the class. They were the inner circle.

Now somebody else was playing the panpipes and Norma and Roger were dancing together. I watched them gloomily. What was going to happen to me when I graduated in June? I guess I'd go on to college, but what then? My mother wanted me to be a doctor, and my father . . . my father drove a bus, and he always said he'd be proud of me whatever I wanted to do. Actually, I figured he'd be just as pleased if I didn't go on to college, if I went out and got a job and relieved him of my share of child support. But he always acted as if he thought I should go to college.

I've got time to make up my mind, my advisor says. He doesn't want me to waste his time sitting around discussing it with him, while all those hordes of students wait to see him. I still don't know what I'm going to do. Sometimes I think that's how I'll spend my life, wondering what I'm going to be doing with it. I get mostly B-s in my classes and that's probably where I'm going to end up in life, being a B- in whatever I do. The only thing I'll ever get an A in is looks.

"Come on, Jeff, dance with me," Dolores said, pulling at my arm.

I stood up, put my arm around her and we started dancing. Dolores was shorter than Norma, and her body felt warm and soft. Suddenly I wondered what the fat girl would feel like, and I wanted to puke.

The fat girl always made a lot of noise whenever she came into class. Usually she was late—maybe because she moved so slowly. The rest of us could usually beat out the bell, darting through the door just as the teacher was about to close it. Ms. Holland yelled at anybody who came late, but when the fat girl lumbered through the door, banging against it and clumping noisily to her seat, she just shook her head.

You always knew the fat girl was there. I always knew she was there. I could hear her heavy breathing when she sat near me on the bench, and it seemed to me she always tried to sit near me. I could smell her too, a fat, sweet smell that made me think of fried bananas. Yuck!

Now she was learning to throw on the wheel and, as usual, Norma was working patiently with her. She was too big, and there wasn't enough room for her to move her legs or her arms. She couldn't seem to center the clay either. Even if Norma did it for her, it invariably collapsed under the weight of her hands as she began pulling it up. Finally, one day in early December, with a lot of help from Norma, she managed to turn an ugly, lumpy bowl about eight inches high. She was proud of it and hovered over it during that week as it moved through drying, bisque firing, and finally glazing. She hung around that afternoon for the kiln to be unloaded, and her face was radiant as she picked up her bowl, covered in a muddy green glaze. She didn't say anything, but she smiled at Norma and hurried away, carrying the ugly little pot with her.

"Poor thing," said Norma. "I don't think she'll ever really learn."

"I hope she's not planning to take ceramics again next term," I said, looking with satisfaction at my two pieces that had come out of the kiln. One was only an ordinary mug. But the other was a low bowl with a golden crackle glaze which, I thought, had an elegance and delicacy far beyond anything I'd done before.

"Lovely," Dolores said, looking over my shoulder. And even Roger whistled.

I held it out toward Norma, and she smiled and nodded but didn't say anything. It seemed to me this bowl represented a breakthrough for me, but Norma kept right on unloading the kiln and chattering away.

"I think she's planning to take ceramics again next term," she said.

"Who?" I turned the bowl in my hands and looked inside to the shimmering golden translucent center, like an open heart.

"Ellen. Ellen De Luca."

"Somebody should tell her."

"Tell her what?"

"That she'd do herself and the rest of us a big favor if she'd go bust up another class. It's a real drag having her around."

The three of them were silent, silent and motionless. They were looking around me to the door of the room. What was there? I didn't want to look. It couldn't be the fat girl. Her entrances were always marked with loud bangs and crashes. And besides, she had taken her ugly pot and gone. It couldn't be the fat girl.

But it was. She was standing there, silently for the first time, holding her pot in one hand and her books in the other. Nobody said anything. She was looking at me, and I knew she'd heard what I had just said. She put down her pot on one of the tables and pulled a tissue out of her pocket. Very, very slowly. We all stood and watched her. Very slowly, she began crying. She moved the tissue up to her eyes in her large fist and began wiping them. Then she turned, crashed against the door, and left.

"Wow!" Roger whispered.

Dolores made a face. "She must have heard."

Norma said angrily to me, "Now look what you've done. You're always going on and on about her. What did she ever do to you? What did she ever do to anybody?"

"I didn't know she was there," I said.

"She always makes a lot of noise," Dolores said. "This was the first time she didn't. Jeff didn't hear her. It wasn't his fault. He didn't mean to make her feel bad."

"It was his fault," Norma shouted. "He never stops saying mean things about her. If you keep saying mean things about a person, sooner or later she'll hear it."

"Look, Norma, I'm sorry."

"A lot of good that's going to do. You made her cry," Norma yelled. "Now do you feel good?"

"No, I feel lousy."

"Well, do something!"

I ran out into the hall, but it was empty. I didn't know which staircase she took, but I hurried down the closest one and out onto the street. What was I going to say to her anyway? "I'm sorry, Fat Girl—I mean Ellen. I'm sorry, Ellen. I don't really think you're a drag."

She wasn't in sight in the street. It would be impossible to miss her if she were. What could I say to her? "Look, Ellen, I'm sorry I said what I did. I didn't mean it."

But I did mean it. I didn't want her in my class next term. I didn't want her watching me and spying on me. And I didn't want her making me angry and cruel. It was all her fault.

I walked slowly upstairs to the ceramics room. Norma was tidying up and refused to look at me.

"I couldn't find her," I said.

The muddy green, misshapen pot was still sitting out on the table where she had left it. I picked it up and held it out to Norma. "Look, she left her pot. I'll put it up on the shelf and tomorrow I'll tell her I'm sorry. Come on, Norma, I didn't know she was there. I wouldn't have said it if I'd known. I'll make it up to her. You'll see."

She was still mad, but after I'd helped her clean off the table and benches, she calmed down and let me come home with her and stay for dinner. Her mother made marinated tofu shish kebobs, but it was a great evening anyway. I didn't get home until nearly midnight, and my mother yelled at me and called me selfish.

five

The fat girl didn't come to school the next day. The ugly little pot sat up there on the shelf unclaimed. Nobody noticed her absence except me. Even Norma seemed to have forgotten about her.

"The fat girl didn't come to class today," I told her.

"Oh no?" She looked around. "Maybe she's sick."

"Maybe," I said. But I didn't think that was the reason.

She wasn't in school on Monday either.

"The fat girl didn't come to class today either," I told Norma.

Norma said impatiently, "Look, Jeff, her name is Ellen. Why don't you call her Ellen?"

"Okay. Ellen didn't come to school today."

"So?"

"So—I wonder why she didn't. I wonder if . . . if it has anything to do with what happened Thursday."

It took Norma a second or two to remember. She was busy brushing delicate scallops around the rim of a low, flared bowl. She put her brush down and looked at me. "Oh, Jeff, I hope it's not because of that."

"What do you think I should do?"

"I don't know. Maybe you could call her and ask how she is. Or maybe—maybe I could call her. Would you like me to call her?"

Her lovely, kind face was filled with pity for Ellen. How I loved Norma! I reached over and pressed her hand. Then I looked at the ugly, green pot on the shelf. "I think maybe I should handle it myself. Maybe I'll just stop at her house and bring her the pot. I don't have to say anything about Thursday. It would be worse if I apologize. I've been thinking about it over the weekend. You were right, Norma. I've been weird and I don't know why. But that's all over now. I'm going to take the pot over to her house. From now on, I'm going to try to . . . to be more friendly to her."

"You're a nice guy, Jeff," Norma said softly. "Did I ever tell you I think you're a nice guy?"

"No, I'm not," I said. "I'm a jerk, but I'm going to be different after this."

I thought about what I was going to say on the way over to her house that afternoon. I was going to be friendly, a little hearty, the way you were supposed to be with the deformed. "Hey, how are things, Ellen? We missed you in class, and I thought I'd drop your cute little pot over. Are you sick? Can I get you anything?" Real cool! I'd make-believe Thursday never happened and, after this, whenever I saw her, I'd smile at her, maybe wink, maybe wave, throw a few crumbs of kindness in her direction.

But it wasn't going to be easy, because I still loathed her. I still hoped she wouldn't take ceramics next term, wouldn't be there watching me, disturbing my balance and, most of all, making me forget that I was a nice guy. Like Norma said, that's what I am, a nice guy. I don't go around making girls cry—not even huge, bloated ones. I'm a nice guy.

"Hi, there, Ellen," I was going to say. "How are things?"

But maybe she would yell at me or slam the door in my face. She shouldn't—she should be grateful—but maybe she wouldn't. You never knew what to expect with a creature like that. Here I was going out of my way to deliver her tacky pot to her, and if she carried on, well, it wouldn't be my fault.

I was getting myself all worked up over her by the time I reached her house. To my surprise, it was a very pretty house. I guess I was expecting that she'd live in a messy, dumpy place. But her house had brown shingles and neat flower boxes filled with red geraniums lining the sides of the stairway. When I rang the bell, I could hear chimes inside. I checked the address Ms. Holland had given me, but it was the right one. A normal-looking boy about twelve opened the door.

"Uh—does Ellen De Luca live here?"

"Uh huh."

"Well, is she home? I'm a—a classmate of hers."

"She's sick."

"Oh, well, I don't want to disturb her, so would you please give her . . ."

"Who is that, Ricky?" came a voice from behind him. And a normal-looking woman came to the door and inspected me.

"I'm Jeff Lyons, Mrs. De Luca, a—a classmate of Ellen's. I just wondered how she was."

"She's been sick," the woman said quickly. Too quickly.

"Well, I don't want to bother her. I just wanted to drop something off."

Mrs. De Luca suddenly smiled at me and opened the door. "Come in, Jeff. I'm sure she'll be glad to see you. She's much better. Nothing contagious."

"She's eating," Ricky said.

"She'll be glad to see you," repeated Mrs. De Luca. "Come in, come in."

Inside, she led me into a bright kitchen filled with plants. Baskets and pretty blue and white dishes hung on one wall. Glass doors led out onto a deck filled with pots of colorful flowers. It was a lovely room, and smack in the center of it sat Ellen, a half-empty plate of cookies in front of her. She looked enormous, dressed in an ugly pink and green flowered wrapper, with lace edging her huge throat.

"Here's a friend of yours, Ellen," said her mother in a hearty voice.

She looked up at me, her fat face impassive, very white but with an unmistakable red rim around the eyes.

"Hi, Ellen," I said cheerily. "How are things?"

Ellen didn't answer. She bent her head over the plate of cookies in front of her. There was a half-empty glass of milk also on the table.

"How about some milk and cookies, Jeff?" said her mother quickly. "I just baked some."

"Thanks a lot, Mrs. De Luca. They smell great, but I had something to eat before I came."

Both of us looked at Ellen, who remained silent, so Mrs. De Luca said, "Why don't you have a seat, Jeff?"

Just then another boy, also a normal-looking one about fourteen or fifteen, wearing a soccer shirt, came into the kitchen and said, "Come on, Mom. I'm late." He took a cookie off the plate in front of Ellen and smiled at me.

"This is my other son, Matt," she said. "I've got to drive him over to the park." She looked in a worried way at Ellen. "Is there anything you want outside, Ellen? I'm going to take Ricky for a pair of tennis shoes, and then I have to pick up a few things at the store. Do you want anything outside?"

Ellen shook her head. She kept her eyes on the plate of cookies.

"Well, dear, I won't be gone too long. It was nice meeting you, Jeff. Help yourself to some milk and cookies if you get hungry."

"Thank you, Mrs. De Luca," I said. "I won't be staying long."

I could hear her talking and laughing with her sons,

the bustle of getting out, the door slamming, the sound of the car starting up, and then silence. Ellen was still looking at the cookies on the table.

"Hey, Ellen," I said. "I'm sorry you're sick. I brought your little pot over, and . . . well, we missed you in class today."

She looked up at me then, and the tears began streaming down her face.

"Hey, Ellen," I said, ". . . listen Ellen, don't cry. Listen . . . I . . . I'm sorry. I didn't mean what I said."

"Yes, you did," she said. "You did mean it."

"No, I didn't," I lied. "It was just a lousy day for me. You know how it is sometimes. You have a lousy day, and you just say stupid things that you don't mean. Honestly, Ellen, I didn't mean it."

"I'm going to kill myself," she said in a flat voice.

I could feel the terror twisting up inside my stomach. I wanted to open the window and yell for help. I wanted to get up and run away from her, away from what she was saying. She was going to kill herself. My God! I didn't even want to be in the same room with her.

"No," I cried, "no, don't . . . ."

"I'm going to kill myself," she repeated.

I wanted to get out of that room as fast as I could.

But I knew I couldn't leave her alone there in the house. Where was her mother? Oh, God! Her mother wouldn't be back until she dropped Matt off at the park, bought Ricky his tennis shoes, and picked up a few things at the store. Maybe a couple of hours. I was all alone with the fat girl in her house, and I was going to have to stay with her until her mother returned, and I was going to have to stop her from killing herself. I was so frightened and so close to bawling myself, I could barely say to her, "Please, Ellen, don't talk like that. Don't! Just because a creep like me says a dumb thing . . ."

"It's not you."

"I didn't mean it, Ellen. Honestly."

"It's everybody else too. Nobody likes me. I'm going to kill myself."

"Don't Ellen! Don't say it!"

"Why not?"

"Nobody should say it. And you're only a kid. Kids shouldn't talk like that. There's all sorts of wonderful things ahead of you to look forward to."

"Like what?"

"Like . . . well . . . like . . ."

Her arm lay on the table, huge and pale like lard. I should've reached out and held those swollen fingers in my hand and showed her I cared about her. A shudder of revulsion ran through me.

Her fat face glistened from all her fat tears. Her nose began running, and she sniffled and snorted and said, "Nobody cares about me."

"Sure they do. Your family . . ."

"They're ashamed of me. My brothers don't want to be seen with me. They don't want anybody to know I'm their sister. Nobody cares about me."

I reached out and took her hand in mine. I felt her hot, clammy, fat fingers in my palm, but I held on. The tears were bouncing off the plate of cookies in front of her. "I'm going to kill myself," she said again, but it sounded different this time, not so fierce, as if it mattered that I was holding her hand. I could feel the panic inside me begin to ease.

"Look, Ellen, stop talking like that. Things are going to be different from now on. Maybe the kids in school haven't been very nice, and maybe I've been a jerk too, but . . ."

"You're not the only one."

"It's going to be different from now on, Ellen," I said very slowly, stalling for time. I looked at the clock over the refrigerator. Only eight minutes had passed. I had at least another hour and three-quarters to go before her mother returned.

She looked at me, and I smiled and squeezed her hand. Then she looked away, as she always did when I caught her watching me. She was embarrassed. Good, I thought, sneaking another look at the clock. Nine minutes gone and all I had to do was stall her until her mother returned. What should I do? Ask her to play cards or Monopoly?

"Why don't you just go and leave me alone," she said.

"I'm not leaving," I told her.

I checked the clock again. Not even ten minutes had passed. I felt exhausted, but I knew I couldn't just get up and leave her alone in that house. As long as I remained, she would stay alive. I didn't want her to die. I didn't want anybody to die, not even the fat girl. I loathed her, loathed her fat, ugly face and the fat, ugly fingers I was holding in my hand. But I didn't want her to die—even if it meant she would be in my ceramics class next term.

"Look," I said, dropping her hand carefully but moving my chair closer, "Promise me you won't do it."

She shook her head but kept her eyes averted.

"Let's just talk to your mother when she gets back."

She snapped her head back. "No! Don't tell my mother.

Promise you won't tell her." Her fat face was flushed a kind of purple, and her pale, little eyes were glittering like small pieces of green Jell-O.

"Okay, okay, Ellen, calm down. Let's make a bargain. I promise not to tell your mother, if you promise not to kill yourself."

"And I don't want you to tell your girlfriend either," Ellen yelled, her face full of blotchy, purple spots. "I don't want her laughing at me. That's what she'll do if you tell her. She'll laugh at me."

"No, no, no, Ellen. You don't know Norma. She would never laugh at you. She likes you. She . . ."

"Well I don't like her, and I want you to promise that you won't tell her. I want you to promise you won't tell her, or my parents, or anybody else."

"Okay, Ellen, I promise. Just calm down."

She did calm down. Then she began talking, while I listened and watched the clock.

"I've never had a friend. Once, in second grade, there was another girl who was fat too. And everybody kept acting like we had to be friends because we both were so fat. I guess I was willing, but she wasn't. She wasn't as fat as me, and she acted even meaner than the others. They didn't like her either, but she would rather sit by herself during lunch than have anybody see her with me. Once she even told me to stop watching her all the time. She always thought I was watching her. But I wasn't. Why would I watch her anyway? If I'm going to watch somebody, it wouldn't be her. It would be . . ."

She hesitated. I tried not to look at the clock.

"It would be somebody good-looking, somebody like you. I know you hated it because I kept watching you. But I didn't mean anything. It was only . . . well . . . I've got my dreams like anybody else. I can't help that. Inside, I'm just like anybody else."

"Sure you are, Ellen. Just don't get so worked up. Here, have a cookie."

I held one out to her, but she shook her head and went on talking, her small, squeaky voice high and shrill.

"Why should you be interested in me? No boy's ever been interested in me. I'm like any other girl inside. I'm nearly seventeen, and I want what everybody my age wants. But there's no way I can have it."

"Sure you can, Ellen," I told her. "People will get to know you, and they'll like you."

She shook her head.

"You knew I was watching you, and I knew you knew and you hated me, but I couldn't help myself. I used to watch you and that girlfriend of yours. I'd see you kissing and making out, and it made me feel good, like I was a part of it. But you hated me, and you gave me all those mean looks, and then you said . . ."

"Look, Ellen, I've been a jerk. Okay? A real jerk, and I'm sorry. It's going to be different from now on. I'm going to be your friend, and Norma's going to be your friend. You'll feel better and you'll have friends and nobody will ever say mean things to you again, because . . . because I won't let them."

Her mother didn't come back for two and a half hours. Ellen stood up and walked with me to the door. "Remember," she whispered, "you promised you wouldn't tell anybody."

"Sure, Ellen," I said. "I remember."

six

From the first phone I could find, I called her house. If Ellen had answered, I would have hung up. Luckily it was her mother.

"Mrs. De Luca, this is Jeff Lyons."

"Who?"

"The boy in Ellen's class. I was just at your house."

"Oh yes, J—"

"No, no, please, Mrs. De Luca! Don't say my name. I don't want Ellen to know I'm calling."

"Oh?"

"Is she there, Mrs. De Luca? I mean, in the same room?"

"No, she's upstairs watching TV. What is it? What's wrong?" Her voice was worried.

"I'm very sorry to tell you this, Mrs. De Luca, but Ellen told me she was going to kill herself."

God, that felt good! Telling her! Getting it off my back and onto hers. Now I'd done my duty, and I could go home and stop worrying about her. Now it was her family's worry. They could lock her up or send her away or do whatever you have to do to stop a nutty, fat girl from committing suicide.

"Oh!" said her mother.

"I feel bad about telling you this, Mrs. De Luca. She made me promise I wouldn't tell you, but I knew you had to know. Maybe you don't have to tell her I told you. And if there's anything I can do . . ."

"Yes, you can, Jeff," said her mother. "Just don't tell anybody."

"No, of course not," I said, "but I knew I should tell you."

"Yes, of course."

"I was afraid she . . ."

Her mother laughed. "She won't. You don't have to be afraid. She's always saying she's going to kill herself. It doesn't mean anything."

"But . . ."

"At least once a day," said her mother, "she says she's going to kill herself. Usually before dinner. But once she gets some food in her, she feels better. And tonight I'm making stuffed breast of veal, one of her favorites, so she should really cheer up."

"She said she was going to do it today, Mrs. De Luca. I was really worried. I'm still worried."

"No, it's fine, Jeff. Believe me. I'm her mother. She doesn't mean it. But it was nice of you to call, and I won't tell her you told me. Goodbye."

I called Norma and told her.

"But there's nothing to worry about, Jeff. You heard what her mother said."

"I know. But you didn't see her when she said she was going to do it. You didn't see how her face turned purple and the words came out between her teeth." The panic began twisting up inside me again. "Suppose she really does it, Norma, suppose she . . . I don't know . . . but suppose she does."

"Jeff! Jeff! Stop worrying. You did what you could. You went over to her house. You spent the afternoon there, and you made her feel good. Then you told her mother. You don't have to worry about a thing."

"Do you really think so, Norma?"

"I really do. And from now on, just be nice to her. I'll try too."

"But don't tell her I told you. I promised I wouldn't tell you. She thinks we laugh at her."

"Of course I won't tell her. And maybe I can get some of the other kids to treat her better."

"I wonder why she said she was going to kill herself if she wasn't going to do it?"

"Maybe she does it to get attention."

"But how can she even say it?"

"She doesn't mean it, Jeff, so it doesn't count."

"No, I guess it doesn't—if she really doesn't mean it."

"And isn't it funny how her mother said she was making breast of veal tonight for dinner and that would cheer her up?"

Norma began laughing and so did I, just as the fat girl said we would.

That night, I woke up so frightened, it was like being five years old all over again. Things crouched there in the darkness around my bed, and I leaped up and ran down the hall to my mother's room. Her door was closed.

The small night-light from the bathroom calmed me down. I leaned, still trembling, against my mother's door and felt the terrors begin to leave. I moved on into the kitchen, snapped on the light and looked at the clock. Only two thirty. It felt much later.

What would she have said, my mother? I grinned foolishly. She would have reasoned with me. She would have spoken slowly, logically, with just an edge of impatience in her voice.

"There is nothing to be afraid of, Jeff."

"But I'm afraid, Mom."

"What are you afraid of, Jeff?"

"I don't know, but I'm afraid."

"You can't be afraid of nothing, Jeff."

"There's something there, Mom. It's going to get me. It's going to kill me."

"There's nothing to be afraid of."

"But I'm afraid."

It was always a draw until she put the lock on the door. And it worked. Up until now. Up until the fat girl.

I hadn't been dreaming about her. She wasn't even in the dream. But when I woke up, I was thinking about her as I'd been thinking about her all through the evening. The fat girl—Ellen—said she wanted to kill herself. She didn't mean it. Her mother said she didn't mean it, and Norma said she didn't mean it. But she said it.

Maybe she wasn't afraid to say it, but I was afraid. I've always been afraid of dying. I don't want to die. I don't even want to think about dying. And I don't want to think about anybody else—even the fat girl—dying.

I opened the refrigerator and inspected the interior. Food—I suddenly needed to eat. You couldn't eat if you were dead, could you? I passed over the four cold artichokes, the leftover pork roast, and reached for the cold mashed potatoes.

"What's the matter, Jeff? Can't you sleep?"

My mother stood in the doorway, watching me eat my cold mashed potatoes.

"I just woke up, Mom, and I guess I was hungry."

My mother nodded and moved up to the table. She didn't have the rumpled look of somebody who had just been awakened.

"I didn't wake you, did I, Mom?"

She shook her head and sat down. "No. I was up. I couldn't sleep."

"Want some?" I indicated the bowl of potatoes.

"God, no! I can't think of anything worse than cold mashed potatoes in the middle of the night." She laughed suddenly, and I swallowed another spoonful and grinned back at her.

"Different strokes for different folks," I said.

"But I am a little hungry." She opened the refrigerator and looked inside. She pulled out a cold artichoke, put it on a plate and joined me at the kitchen table. We both munched away for a while in a comfortable, friendly way.

"Mom," I said, "can I ask you something?"

Her teeth made sharp, little parallel lines in the artichoke petal. "Sure, Jeff, what is it?"

"Did you ever work with people who said they were going to commit suicide?"

"Not recently. But when I was younger, I worked on a psychiatric ward, and some of the patients threatened to kill themselves."

"And did they?"

"Some of them did," said my mother, picking up the heart of the artichoke and biting off a small piece.

"But . . . do most of them . . . I mean, if people say they will . . ."

My mother swallowed the last bit of artichoke, daintily licked her fingers with her small, pink tongue and looked at me. "Why are you so interested, Jeff?"

"I'd just like to know, Mom."

"Is it for a school report?"

"No."

"Well . . ." She was looking worried now. "That's not what's keeping you up, is it, Jeff?"

"I guess it is, Mom. I know somebody who says she's going to kill herself."

She was still looking at me. I thought to myself, Why don't I tell her about Ellen? I was bursting with it, and I wanted to tell my mother. I wanted to share it with her like we were sharing the quiet kitchen in the middle of the night, sharing a good, close feeling that we never usually had during the day. Maybe after I told her about Ellen, I could even tell her how scared I was that night. Maybe she'd laugh when I told her, and then I'd laugh, and then she'd say, "It's not so terrible to be afraid."

"Jeff?"

"What is it, Mom?"

She was still looking at me, a troubled look on her face.

"It's not Wanda you're talking about, is it? It's not Wanda who says she's going to kill herself?"

"No, Mom, it has nothing to do with Wanda."

"You're sure, Jeff? You're not trying to hide anything from me?"

"Mom, I swear it has nothing to do with Wanda. It's

this fat girl in my class. Why do you keep worrying it's Wanda?"

"Because suddenly she seems to be going through some kind of stage or other. And there's something else. She hasn't said anything to you, has she?"

"About what?"

"About what's bothering her. She . . . she's been going over to your father's house a lot. Suddenly. She hasn't done that in years."

"Dad's house? Wanda's been going to Dad's house?"

My mother's face showed relief at my surprise. She bent closer toward me over the table and lowered her voice. "You know I don't like to nag you or butt into your relationship with your father. I don't ask any questions, and I don't expect you to tell me anything. I don't even want to hear anything about him. You know, Jeff, I don't pry."

"I know, Mom." I patted her hand. My mother was grateful. She turned her hand over and took mine. We sat there over the kitchen table, holding hands and whispering.

"But I do like to know where you both are, especially Wanda. After all, she's only fourteen and a girl."

"Sure, Mom. That's right, Mom."

"So a couple of times this past month, she made-believe she was over at her friend Marcie's house for dinner.

Maybe it happened even more than that, but two times I know she said she was at Marcie's when she was really over at your father's."

"But why, Mom, why wouldn't she tell you the truth?"

"I don't know, but I'm worried."

I squeezed her hand and told her not to worry. I told her it probably was a stage Wanda was going through, but I knew why Wanda wasn't telling her the truth. Because Wanda couldn't stand seeing the misery and jealousy on my mother's face. Just like I couldn't stand it.

But for now, we were both relaxed and comfortable, and I wasn't going to spoil it.

"She never said anything to you, Jeff, did she?"

"No, Mom, she didn't. Do you want me to ask her?"

"No. I guess we'd better leave her alone. But how about you? Have you been seeing your father lately?"

"You remember. At the beginning of November, I borrowed the car, and Wanda and I went over for dinner. That was the last time. I guess I'll go again during Christmas."

"Go as often as you like, Jeff," said my mother stiffly. "It doesn't matter one bit to me."

"I know that, Mom," I lied.

She bent over and kissed me. After that, we both felt so embarrassed we didn't know where to look.

"I guess we ought to get some sleep," she murmured.

"I guess so."

She yawned. "Well, I'm pretty sleepy now. How about you?"

"Me too, I guess."

"Good night, Jeff. Don't worry about the dishes. Let's just leave them in the sink."

"Good night, Mom."

I fell asleep holding on tight to the good feeling between my mother and myself. Maybe I could talk to her about Ellen tomorrow.

Wanda was full of smiles at the breakfast table the next morning.

"God, I'm hungry today," she said, nibbling on a piece of toast.

"How about an egg?" my mother asked. "I'll make you an egg if you want it."

"No thanks, Mom." Wanda beamed at her. "Your hair looks nice. I think I like it longer."

"I was thinking of getting it cut."

"No, no, why don't you let it grow? You look so . . . so pretty with it long."

I paused over my orange and stared at her. It wasn't like Wanda to be cheerful in the morning. No wonder my mother was uneasy.

She left most of her toast on her plate as she usually did, stood up and said, "Oh, by the way, Mom, I won't be home for dinner tonight. I'm going to Marcie's. We're going to study together."

My mother and I looked at each other.

"I'll pick you up," my mother said.

"No, that's all right. Marcie's father will drop me."

"I'll pick you up," my mother insisted.

Wanda was still smiling. She didn't sense the trap being baited.

"I don't know what time we'll be finished, so . . ."

"I'll call you about ten."

"No, don't call."

"Why not?"

"Because . . . because . . ."

"Because," said my mother, "because you're not going to be at Marcie's house. Because you're lying."

Wanda sat down and looked desperately at me for support.

"The last time you said you were at Marcie's house, I was looking out the window when your father dropped you off. And the time before that, the same thing happened. I saw him drop you off at the corner."

"You're spying on me," Wanda shrieked. "What right do you have to spy on me?" Wanda was a shrewd fighter, quick to change directions when cornered and mount an attack herself. But it didn't work this time.

"Why are you lying, Wanda?" my mother said, her little face all twisted up in pain. It made me hate Wanda, but I swallowed some cold cereal and kept quiet.

Wanda burst into tears.

"You don't have to lie to me," said my mother gently in her suffering voice. "I don't care if you go to your father's house. He is your father. It's only right you should visit him. I only want to know where you are because I'm your mother and I love you."

"Leave me alone!" Wanda shrieked. "Leave me alone!"

"Now stop it, Wanda," I yelled. "You've got no right worrying Mom like that. You should be ashamed of yourself."

"You get off my back, Jeff," Wanda yelled back. "You're never home yourself. It's like a morgue here. And she's always at me, picking at me and complaining, whatever I do. It's no fun. It's fun there. And they like me to come. Linda says she needs another woman in the house. And today's Sean's birthday, and I was going to help with the kids' party in the afternoon. And then at night we were all going out to a Mexican restaurant for dinner. It's fun there. . . I like to go there."

"Sean's birthday?" I said. "I didn't know it was Sean's birthday."

"You don't know anything," Wanda yelled. "You're so wrapped up in Norma, you can't think of anything else."

"But . . . but . . . they never told me. They didn't invite me."

"Now look here, Wanda," said my mother very slowly, very stiffly. "I just want you to tell me where you're going. If you're happier with your father . . ."

"I didn't say that, did I?" Wanda shouted.

"If you're happier with your father . . ."

"Yes, yes, yes! I am happier with him. I hate it here! I hate it!" Wanda jumped up and ran out of the room.

My mother and I sat together over the table, just as we had a few hours before. I could feel the misery and the hurt radiating out from her, but I was feeling pretty hurt myself. They were going to celebrate Sean's birthday that night, and nobody invited me. It was true that I had declined most of their invitations in the past, but my father had always dutifully extended them. How come he hadn't this time?

"I told you," said my mother. "You see? I told you."

"Wanda's a pain," I told her. "She never thinks of anybody but herself."

"She's not happy here."

I shrugged my shoulders. "She'll get over it."

My mother stood up and began gathering the dishes. "She's happier there than here. You heard what she said."

"Oh, Mom," I said, "don't make a big deal out of it. She's just going to Sean's birthday party. She always likes to go to parties. Everybody likes to go to parties."

"You too, Jeff?" My mother was looking at me. I could feel it coming on, but there was no way of stopping it. There never was any way of stopping it.

"He didn't ask me," I told her.

"Well, I'm sure you could go if you wanted to," said my mother, turning her back. "I'm sure they would be very happy if you went."

"I don't want to go," I said to her back.

She was stacking dishes in the sink, scraping the breakfast bits into the garbage disposal unit.

"Why not, Jeff? Why don't you go too? I could hear from the way you were talking before that you really wanted to go. Why shouldn't you go? I'm sure you'd have a very good time if you went."

Very soon we were shouting at each other, and she was telling me that I was just like my father and that I was selfish. It wasn't until I arrived at school that I remembered I'd forgotten all about Ellen.

seven

She came in late as she usually did, banging against the doorway, dropping her books and clumping noisily to her seat. I tried to catch her eye to smile at her, but she didn't look in my direction. Later, when I managed to get over to her and said, "Hi, Ellen, how are you?" she turned away and didn't answer. I knew her mother had told her about my phone call.

Norma went out of her way to heap attention and praise on her. She worked with her at the wheel and kept saying cheerily, "That's great, Ellen, keep it up. You're really getting there. Keep it up."

She must have said something to Dolores and Roger

too because they came over to observe, and you could hear their encouraging voices mingling with Norma's.

I couldn't work. I was too busy watching the fat girl.

She couldn't work either. All the attention being heaped on her made her even more clumsy than usual. Her pot collapsed on the wheel. And when Norma urged her to try another, she just shook her head, not looking at Norma, not looking at any of the kids standing around the wheel, cheering her on. It was horrible, and I felt responsible.

"I'll talk to you later," I told Norma when the bell rang, and I hurried after the fat girl.

"Ellen!" I called out. "Ellen, wait a second!"

She kept right on moving, her head down. I caught up with her and said, "Listen, Ellen, I want to explain."

"Go away," she said. "I don't want to talk to you."

"I know you're sore," I said, looking at her face, trying to get her to look at mine.

"But I really was worried about you."

"You promised," she said, still moving, still keeping her face down, "and you're a liar. You told my mother. You told everybody. Go away! I hate you!"

"I was worried about you, Ellen. That's why I called

your mother. I didn't want anything to happen to you. I didn't know . . ."

"What didn't you know?" Ellen's head snapped up, and she was glaring at me now, her little green eyes fierce.

"Look, Ellen, I really want to be your friend. Where are you going now?"

She didn't answer.

"Is this your last class? It's mine and if you're free, maybe we can go someplace and talk."

"I have to go home."

"Well, can I walk with you?"

"No."

"How about later then?"

She shook her head.

"I know. How about coming out for a pizza with me later? How about that, Ellen, just the two of us? I really want to talk to you. Come on, Ellen, let's go to Vince's later and have a pizza. They have the best pepperoni pizza in the city. You'll like their pizza. I always get them to add extra cheese . . ."

I was jabbering on and on, but I could see her hesitating. Food, that was the way to get to her. Food.

"Or we could have him make up Vince's Special with Italian sausage, mushrooms, anchovies . . ."

She was looking at me now, her head slightly tilted, considering. Was she wondering what her mother was cooking for dinner that night? What she'd be missing if she had pizza with me?

"I mean, if you like pizza, we could go to Vince's. Otherwise, we could go someplace else."

"I like pizza," she said solemnly.

"Good. I'll pick you up about six. Is six okay?"

She nodded slowly.

"Well, that's fine then, Ellen. I'll see you later."

When I told Norma I was taking the fat girl out for pizza that night, her eyes filled with tears.

"You're a nice guy, Jeff. Did I ever tell you that before?"

"I'm a jerk, Norma, and I've really screwed things up for the fat . . . I mean, Ellen. From now on, I'm always going to call her Ellen."

"Well, don't be too hard on yourself. She has to take some responsibility too for what's happening to her."

"You're right, Norma, and maybe I can tell her so. I mean, I don't want it to be too heavy. But maybe if she feels I'm really interested in what happens to her, and she can trust me, maybe I can help her."

"It should be some evening," Norma said, smiling. "I'll be interested in hearing all about it."

And that's when it really started—the end, I mean. Because I felt myself growing angry. But at what? At the way she was smiling? At the way she assumed I was going to tell her everything that passed between Ellen and myself?

"And another thing, Norma," I said, trying to keep the irritation out of my voice. "You don't have to lay it on so thick with her. I mean, it's great that you're trying to be friendly, and I know you told Roger and Dolores to be nice too, but you don't have to bury her in it."

She didn't notice my irritation. She was a person who could always take criticism without snapping back. She just nodded and said, "You're right, Jeff. I guess I was too obvious." And then she kissed me and I kissed her, and the beginning of the end got lost for a while.

My mother worked the seven thirty to three thirty shift at her job, so the two of us got home around the same time. She was unloading some packages from the car, and I helped her carry them up the stairs. The phone was ringing as we entered the apartment. It was my father.

"Hello, Jeff."

"Oh, hi, Dad." I was using the phone in the kitchen,

and I watched as my mother set down her package and walked out of the room.

"I'm glad I got you, Jeff. I meant to call you last night, but David fell down the stairs and needed a few stitches in his leg, so . . ."

"How is he now?"

"He's fine. He's fine, but that's why I didn't call you."

"I'm glad he's okay."

"Well, the thing is, I wanted to tell you that Sean's having a birthday party this afternoon, just with some of the kids in the neighborhood. But tonight we're all going out to dinner, and I'd like you to come too. I would have called you last night . . ." His voice sounded awkward. Wanda must have told him.

"That's okay, Dad. I can't come anyway."

"You know, Jeff, you're always invited to any family party here. I wouldn't want you to feel . . ."

"It's okay. I'm going out with a friend tonight for pizza."

"With Norma? Well, look, why don't the two of you come along with us? I haven't met Norma yet, but I'd like to. Wanda told us all about her, and you can bring her too."

"No, it's not Norma, and I don't think I can. It's somebody else who's got some problems, and we need to talk."

"Well, I'm sorry, Jeff. I really meant to call you yesterday. I don't want you to feel left out. You know you're my number-one son." He was trying to be funny, and it embarrassed both of us.

"I know, Dad. It's okay. I don't feel left out."

"How about coming over another day this week? We never see you. Why don't you bring Norma over for dinner one night?"

"Well . . ."

"Come on, Jeff."

"Okay, Dad."

"When?"

"Well, how about Friday? If she can make it."

"Or Saturday or Sunday. Any night's fine, and Linda and the kids will be so happy. Just let me know."

"Okay, Dad, and wish Sean a happy birthday from me. And give my best to Linda."

"I will, Jeff. Thanks. And you know, I really would have called you last night."

"I know, Dad."

I was exhausted when I hung up the phone. My

mother returned to the kitchen as soon as I stopped talking, and began unpacking the groceries.

"Mom," I asked, "can I have the car tonight?"

"Of course," she said stiffly. I knew she was thinking I needed the car to go to Dad's house.

"I'm not going to Dad's house," I told her, "because I have a date with somebody in my ceramics class. Not exactly a date, but I'm taking somebody out for pizza, and I'd like the car."

She piled a few tuna fish cans in the closet but didn't say anything. I knew she thought I was lying to her, like Wanda, so I explained.

"I'm taking a fat girl named Ellen out for pizza tonight, because I'm sorry for her and I want to help her. She's the one who says she's going to commit suicide. I started telling you about her last night."

My mother brightened up and I went on.

"She keeps saying she's going to kill herself, but her mother says she isn't. Her mother says she's always threatening to kill herself. At least once a day, her mother says, but after a good dinner she generally feels better."

My mother shook her head, but she was smiling. "When people say they're going to kill themselves, you have to take them seriously," she said. "It sounds to me like that's a family who could use some counseling."

My mother handed me the keys to the car and offered to give me some money if I was short.

We ordered an extra-large Vince's Special and waited about fifteen minutes before it arrived. Since it was Tuesday night, the place wasn't mobbed the way it always was on weekends. Still, Danny Ryan and his girlfriend, Amy Peterson, were there, sitting at a table on the other side of the room. "Hey, Jeff," Danny called out when we came in. But then he blinked hard and his smile kind of stuck on his face when he saw Ellen. Amy turned around to stare and gave me such a wide, phony smile, I could feel the irritation growing inside me again. Very deliberately, I rested my arm on Ellen's shoulder as I guided her over to a table.

She didn't notice. She was busy sniffing the air as we waited for our pizza. Her eyes rested hungrily on all the dishes that could be seen on adjoining tables. She was dressed up in another one of her old-lady outfits.

"I've never been here before," she said. "When we go out for pizza, we usually go to John's or Ernesto's."

"I think this is the best place in the city."

She smiled and nodded at me. Good! She wasn't angry anymore.

"Anyway, Ellen, I wanted to explain about yesterday, and I wanted to apologize. I know I promised not to tell your mother, but I was afraid you would, you would . . ."

Her face grew serious. "Kill myself? I will, too."

"Now Ellen, don't start that all over again."

"I know *she* told you I wouldn't. SHE doesn't believe me. *She* thinks I won't do it, but I will." She was pouting like a little child.

"Look, Ellen, that's what I wanted to talk about. Has your family ever gone for counseling?"

"Counseling?" Ellen screwed up her face and twitched her nose as if something smelled bad. "Ever since I can remember, either we're all going, or I'm going, or my parents are going, or my brothers. Right now, my mother and Ricky are going, but I'm not going anymore."

"But maybe you should."

"Why?"

"Maybe it will make you feel better."

"I'm never going to feel better until I'm dead," she said. "I just can't make up my mind how to do it. The best way is to jump off the bridge, but I don't know how I'd get myself out there. I don't drive. I could take the

29 bus, but then I'd have to walk and I'm not really sure I'd like to jump off the bridge. I think it would hurt too much. I don't want it to hurt. I could cut my wrists. That might be the easiest way, but blood makes me throw up. So I guess I'll have to take sleeping pills, but then somebody might find me . . ."

She went on and on, and I listened. I meant to talk to her about going for counseling, and I meant to say something about changing her attitudes and making friends, but that night I forgot everything, listening to her. I was fascinated as she talked on and on, listing all the possible ways she was considering killing herself.

She stopped talking when the pizza came and she began eating. I talked a little then, but she barely listened. She ate slowly, with deep concentration. Maybe I ate two or three pieces. She ate all the rest.

eight

That night it happened again. I woke up so frightened I could barely get my arm out from beneath the blanket to flip on the lamp next to my bed. Even with the light on, I could feel it pressing in on me. I knew it was because of Ellen.

The next day I walked her home from school. I talked and this time she listened. It was just before the Christmas break, and the stores and houses that we passed shone with bright ornaments.

"You have to stop talking about killing yourself," I told her. "You have to think about living."

She shook her head.

"You have to find ways to enjoy your life," I insisted. She shook her head again.

"You have to make your life better," I told her, "and you're not going to feel better about yourself until you lose some weight."

"I can't," she said.

"Why can't you? Is it something glandular? Is it a physiological thing?"

"No. I'm just hungry all the time."

"Hobbies," I told her. "You need hobbies. You need to take your mind off food. You have to join clubs. Do you belong to anything at school?"

"No."

"Why not?"

"There's nothing I'm interested in."

"Come on, Ellen, there's got to be something you're interested in."

She had a guilty look on her face, so I said, "I mean, besides food. What do you like to do?"

"I like to watch TV."

"And?"

"Sometimes I like to read."

"And?"

"Well . . . I did get interested in ceramics, but . . .

well . . . I guess I'm not good at it. I thought maybe I could be good at it, but you see . . ."

"No, I don't see," I lied. "Why shouldn't you try? You could go over to the museum. They give courses after school or on weekends. Or you could study with a professional potter like Ida O'Neill. She's the one Roger studied with, so I know she gives lessons."

Ellen's face scrunched up thoughtfully.

"Maybe if you worked at it a little more—on your own, I mean. Maybe if you took some private lessons with a real good potter. After all, Ms. Holland isn't that good. Norma, Roger, and Dolores are much better than she is, and she's kind of disorganized anyway. Why don't you go and take lessons with Ida O'Neill?"

"Maybe," Ellen said. "Maybe I will."

When we reached her house, she hesitated and then said, "Do you want to come in?"

"I'd like to," I told her, "but I work at the hardware store on Mondays and Wednesdays."

She looked away and began speaking very quickly. "Well there's something else I want to ask you. It's my birthday Sunday, and my mother is making dinner, and I thought if you wanted to come, she said I could invite a friend, but if you're busy . . ."

"No," I told her, "I'm not busy. I'd like to come. What time?"

She looked at me then with such a soapy, gooey, worshipful look, I had to turn away. It was the kind of look that was okay for a dog, but not for a human being.

But I smiled at her and patted her on the arm and went off, feeling embarrassed but happy too.

Norma called me that night. "What's been happening with you, Jeff? I haven't had a chance to talk to you in days."

"I've been busy, Norma."

"Well, what happened yesterday?"

"What do you mean?"

"You know what I mean, dummy. With Ellen De Luca? And then I know you walked her home today, so you're really being the Good Samaritan."

"I don't want to talk about it,," I said, feeling irritated again. "I really don't. Can we just forget about Ellen?"

She shut up for a minute and then she said softly, "Okay, Jeff, if you promised her you wouldn't say anything, it's okay with me."

"It's not that . . ."

"You're just a real nice guy, Jeff. Even nicer than I thought. Not many people would take the trouble . . ."

"Let's just drop the whole subject," I snapped. "Just drop it!"

"Okay, Jeff," she agreed, "but if I can do anything at all . . ."

I wanted to hang up on her. Why couldn't she just get off my back? I didn't want her helping me with Ellen. I didn't want anybody helping me with Ellen.

"Let's change the subject, Norma," I said quickly. "I forgot to ask you if you'd come with me to my father's house this Friday. He's invited us both to dinner. I couldn't get out of it, but if you'd rather not go, I'd understand."

"It's fine with me, Jeff. I'd like to meet your father."

Norma brought a couple of jars of pickled watermelon rind, and Linda acted like she was overjoyed to get them. I've never really liked Linda. I know my father's happy with her, and she tries hard to make friends with me, maybe too hard. She's always asking me what I think, and she agrees with whatever I say. I guess she's pretty in a large, blonde, smiley way.

They live in a little house over in the Sunset district. Linda isn't much of a housekeeper—not as bad as Norma's mother, but all the furniture looks scuffed and worn, and there's usually a clutter of kids' toys, sweaters, and newspapers lying around.

Sean and David were looking out of the windows when we drove up Friday night, and they came tearing out the door before we even got out of the car.

"What darlings!" Norma said.

It took only a few minutes for them to get over their shyness with her. David is five and Sean seven. They're cute kids. I don't mind them as much as I do Linda.

"How are you, Jeff?" said my father, giving me a manly handshake and a quick hug.

Norma giggled when she saw him. "You and Jeff look so much alike, Mr. Lyons," she said. "It really is something."

My father liked Norma. So did Linda. So did the boys. They sat on either side of her during dinner and talked to her both at the same time. I sat near Linda and struggled through a typical conversation.

"So what's going on, Jeff?"

"Nothing much."

"Are you still working in the hardware store?"

"On Monday and Wednesday afternoons and every other Saturday."

"Well, I was just telling your father that he ought to

go down and get a new showerhead for the bathroom. I thought maybe you could suggest a better one than the one we have. It's never worked right."

"I don't know anything about showerheads."

"I thought you could show him what you had and maybe tell him which one you think might be best. I don't mind spending a little more."

"I don't know anything about showerheads, Linda."

"Well, I'm sure you know more than he does."

It was rough going. After dinner, Norma helped Linda with the dishes and my father and I went into the living room and looked at each other helplessly. Bad as it was talking with Linda, it was even worse talking to my father when we were by ourselves. When the kids were around it wasn't so bad, but now they were both in the kitchen. You could hear their high, excited little-kid voices.

"That's a nice girl you got there, Jeff."

"Thanks, Dad."

"She's real sweet."

"Mmm."

"Nice looking too, but that's not really important."

"No, I guess not."

"So what's new?"

"Nothing much."

"We don't see you very much these days."

"I know, Dad, but I'm real busy. There's school and my job at the hardware store, and I have to help Mom around the house."

My father leaned forward and said in a low voice, "Jeff, there's something I want to talk to you about."

"What is it?"

"Well, it's Wanda. She's not happy."

"When is Wanda ever happy?" I laughed.

My father went on slowly. "She wants to move in with us."

"With you?"

"Yes. She says she's not happy with your mother."

He was watching me, waiting for me to say something. From the kitchen Sean's voice yelled, "Norma, look at me! Look at me!"

"It's not fair," I said to my father.

He leaned back and his large, handsome face looked worried.

"It's not fair," I repeated. "Mom would go to pieces if Wanda moved out."

My father said carefully, "I know it won't be easy for her, but she's got her job and you'd still be there. I do have to think about what's best for Wanda."

"It's kind of late for that, isn't it?" I snapped.

"Jeff! Jeff!" he said sadly. "You know, Jeff, I tried. But it didn't work. It nearly killed me to leave you kids."

"And what about her?" I said. "What about Mom? Her whole life is the two of us. You've got another family. You've got other kids. You're married. You're happy."

I could hear myself talking at him. Attacking him. I could hear myself sounding just like my mother.

"I know how you feel. I know you're going to take her side. It's only right. I know . . ."

"You don't know anything," I yelled at him. "You don't know what a lousy life she has and what a rotten thing it would be if Wanda moved out."

"Just let me tell you something," my father said, leaning forward. "I don't want to say anything about your mother. She does the best she can, and she's a good woman, but . . . And listen, Jeff, let me talk and don't get excited. She can't help herself, and I know she tries. But I tried too. We were married for eight years, and I got to thinking that life wasn't worth living. Nothing I did made any difference. She was miserable and I was miserable. So I left, and—sure, Linda and I fight sometimes, but it's good now just being alive. And when I hear Wanda talking, when she cries and says she's miserable, what can I do? I'm her father. I have to try and help her, don't I, Jeff?"

I didn't say anything. My father watched me for a while. Then he said, "You too, Jeff. I'm your father too. If you ever needed me . . ."

"I'm fine," I told him. "I'm fine."

"But Wanda isn't," he said. "And I'd like her to live with me, if that's what she wants."

"Mom has custody," I told him. But I knew she wouldn't stop Wanda if she wanted to go. My father knew that too.

"I thought maybe you could talk to your mother."

"Not me," I told him. "I'm not getting involved. I think Wanda's a louse, and if she wants to move out, she'll have to handle it herself."

"Okay, Jeff," said my father. He patted my arm and began talking about football.

"Your father's very nice," Norma told me as we drove home. "That's the way you'll look when you're his age. And the boys are darling. I promised them we'd come and take them to the zoo one day."

"Mmm."

"And Linda's very sweet and friendly. She's such a good mother. I bet she never loses her temper."

"Mmm."

"What's the matter, Jeff? Is something wrong?"

I told her. "Wanda wants to move out. She says she's not happy. My father told me tonight. He wants me to talk to my mother."

"So—will you?"

"Are you kidding? Do you know what will happen to my mother if Wanda leaves?"

Norma put an arm around my shoulder. "Poor Jeff," she said. "Poor Jeff."

"It's not me," I told her. "It's my mother."

"Well," said Norma, "it's easy to see why Wanda wants to move in with them. They're a really happy family."

"But Wanda has some responsibilities too," I said. "My mother's the one who's taken care of her all these years. My father just took off and did his own thing, while my mother was stuck with the two of us."

"Wanda's only fourteen, Jeff, and if she's really unhappy . . ."

"It's not fair," I said. "It's just not fair."

"Poor Jeff!" Norma said.

She wasn't any help. When we got to her house, I told her I was too tired to come upstairs with her, and I could see the hurt in her face. I didn't care. I wanted to hurt her. I wanted to hurt everybody—my father, Linda, Sean, David, Wanda, and my mother too. I knew I was going to wake up scared again that night, and I did. I ate some leftover macaroni and I remembered the doglike look in Ellen's eyes. I began to feel better.

nine

I had worked up quite a speech to lay on Wanda, but none of it turned out as I had expected.

She was ready for me. I guess she'd spoken with my father and had spent some time on her own rehearsing a speech for me. We traded a few whispered words back and forth the next morning, and then I said to my mother, who was washing some sweaters, "Mom, Wanda and I have to go over to the library today. Can we borrow the car?"

"The library?" said my mother. "Over on Anza?"

"No—we have to go down to the main library. But we'll be back in a couple of hours."

"Okay," said my mother. "I need to go shopping later, so don't stay out too long."

We parked the car at Stow Lake and sat inside, watching a couple with a little girl feeding the ducks. The little girl kept putting the bread crumbs into her mouth.

"Do you remember when Dad used to take us here to feed the ducks?" Wanda asked.

"Both of them," I told her. "I remember coming here with Mom and Dad."

"Yes," said Wanda, "but Mom used to sit on the bench and read a magazine. And Dad let us feed the ducks, and sometimes he used to take us rowing."

"Okay, Wanda," I said, "let's talk."

"Fine," she said. "I'm ready."

I told her what I thought. I told her I thought she had a responsibility to Mom and I reminded her that ever since the divorce, it was Mom who'd taken care of us and whose whole life centered around us. I told her that I knew Dad loved us. I didn't want to say anything about Dad. But she had to remember that Dad had another family now, and that Mom only had us.

"I know that," Wanda said impatiently.

I tried to stay calm. "I'm not saying things are perfect at home, Wanda. I know Mom can be difficult, but it's not fair to just walk out on her after all the years she's looked after you."

Wanda looked right at me, her dark, little face defiant.

"You too," she said. "Don't forget she's looked after you too."

"I'm not forgetting, Wanda," I said. "I know I have a responsibility to Mom. I'll always have a responsibility to her."

"That's right," she said, "but you'll be graduating this June and going off to college. I'll be all alone with her. I don't want to be all alone with her. I can't stand it if I have to be alone with her."

"How can you talk like that?" I said.

"It's easy," she came right back at me. "Just like it's easy for you to tell me how to act. You'll be going away in the fall, and as it is, you're never home anyway. You're always away, and I'm the one who's stuck with Mom. So don't go telling me about my responsibilities."

I should have expected that Wanda would attack. It's very seldom that you can get her at bay. I looked through the car window at the little girl with her face all covered with bread crumbs, and I didn't know what to say next.

Wanda put a hand on my arm. Her voice was kindly. "It's not like I'm going to Siberia," she said. "I'll just be across the park. I can spend a night or two with her during the week from time to time, and maybe we can get together over the weekend. She'll get used to it. Maybe she'll even be happy once I go. We fight all the time as it is."

I shook my head. "She won't be happy."

"No, I guess not," said Wanda. "No matter what happens, she'll never be happy. You know that, Jeff. There's nothing we can do. You'll be going away to school, and I . . . I've got to look out for myself. I don't want to be like her, Jeff. I want to have fun and feel good."

"But can't you wait?" I said. "Maybe after I'm gone, maybe after a few months . . ."

"Uh uh, Jeff," my sister said. "I'm not waiting. It'll be better now. You're still home. You'll be home until September. It will give her time to get used to being alone. It would be worse if I waited."

"How do you know you'll like it with Dad?" I asked her. "They live in such a tiny house and the place is a mess."

"Well, maybe I can help. I've learned a lot from Mom, even though she never lets me do anything important. I'm a good cook, and I can help Linda with the housework. Dad says the boys can move in together for a while and I can have Sean's room. Dad's going to fix up the back of the basement and put in another room and a bathroom. So maybe after a year or so, I can take that . . ." She went chirping on and on.

It was funny how upset I was. I hated the thought of Wanda moving out—not only for Mom, but for me too. Wanda belonged to me. She was my drippy kid sister who took at least two showers a day, clogged up the drain with her hair, and whined all the time. But she was part of my territory. I didn't want her to move out. I didn't want to lose something else that belonged to me.

"Listen, Wanda," I tried again. "Maybe we can work out some kind of compromise. Maybe I can try to spend more time at home with Mom. How about you spending every other weekend with Dad?"

Wanda shook her head.

"Okay, how about every weekend? I'll spend more time at home with Mom. I'll try to run a little more interference for you."

Wanda kept on shaking her head.

"Wanda, I really don't want you to go. You're my sister, and . . . I'll miss you. You're a pest, but I don't want you to go."

I tried laughing when I said it and she stopped shaking her head.

"Jeff," she said finally, "I can't stay. I'll miss you too.

I guess I wasn't thinking that you won't be there either. I guess I forgot about you. But you'll be going away soon, and I'd have to stay home alone with her. I can't do it. I'm sorry, but I can't."

Now she was crying and I began crying too. We sat there in the car, looking out at the ducks in Stow Lake, and we cried together.

But the only thing we agreed on was that she wouldn't say anything more about moving out until after Christmas. That she wouldn't spoil the holidays for Mom.

I stayed home that Saturday. Usually I'm either working at the hardware store or out with my friends. My mother does her heavy cleaning on Saturdays, and all I'm ever supposed to do is keep my room neat. Whenever my mother gets angry at me, she says that I don't help around the house. But actually she never really lets me do very much. That day I tried.

"What can I do to help, Mom?" She was washing down the fixtures in the kitchen.

"Just keep out of my way, Jeff."

"Do you want me to vacuum, Mom?"

"No," she said. "You always miss all the corners when you vacuum."

"I'll be careful, Mom."

"Well, okay," she said doubtfully.

Later she ran the vacuum over all the areas I had done earlier.

I offered to help her shop. She declined. "What's the matter, Jeff? How come you're not out with your friends?"

"I thought I'd hang around the house and help you, Mom. You're always saying I don't do enough. So I thought I'd grant you your wish."

She smiled at me. She was in a good mood that day. "You must be feeling guilty or something."

"Uh uh, Mom, my conscience is clear."

"Money?"

"Nope."

"Well—that's all right then. You did your duty. Dismissed!"

"Actually, Mom, I'm free until tonight. Norma and I are going to a movie. What are you doing tonight?"

My mother cocked her head to one side and inspected me. "So that's it—you want the car? Well, you usually can count on it for Saturday night. You know that. I'll be home with Wanda, unless she's going to a friend's. You can have the car, Jeff."

I wanted to ask her why she was always home Saturday nights. Why she never went out with friends. Both of my grandparents were dead, but my Aunt Lisa, Mom's younger sister, and her husband lived over in Kensington. The trouble was that she and Mom weren't talking to each other this year. Some years they talked to each other, and some years they didn't. But there were other relatives as well.

"What ever happened to that uncle of yours, Mom? Uncle Charles?"

"Oh, he's in an old-age home. I should go out and see him sometime."

"And Mom, what about those cousins of yours, the two brothers?"

"Roger and Bill Porter? I don't like Roger's wife. And Bill, well, he's moved again, I think, and I don't know where he is."

There were no men in my mother's life. Danny Lefferts, whose parents are divorced, complains all the time because his mother always brings different boyfriends home to spend the night. I don't think my mother ever even went out with a man since the divorce. It always made me feel relieved that she didn't. But now I worried about what was going to happen to her when Wanda left, and later, when I went off to college. It gave me a heavy, empty feeling just thinking about it, and I wanted to make it up to her in advance. I wanted to make her happy now, so in those lonely days ahead maybe she could remember.

"Hey, Mom, how about coming to the movies with Norma and me? If Wanda wants to come, she can come too."

My mother looked at me nervously.

"Why?" she said.

"Oh, I just thought it might be fun. We haven't gone out together for a long time. I thought maybe you'd like to."

"Thanks, Jeff," said my mother stiffly, "but I'd rather not."

"Why not?"

"What is it, Jeff?" said my mother. "What's wrong?"

"Nothing's wrong."

"So why are you acting so strange?"

"What's strange about asking you to come to a movie with me tonight?"

"And Norma?"

"Well, all right, Norma too."

"Boys don't usually invite their mothers along to chaperone them on dates, do they?"

"Well, I just felt I'd like you along tonight, Mom. I don't think it's strange. You always twist everything I say."

Naturally, it ended in a fight, and I went storming out of the house.

I spent the afternoon shopping for a birthday present for Ellen. I didn't know anything about her—what kind of books she read, the kind of music she liked. I couldn't even remember if she wore jewelry. I ended up buying her a scarf. It was a green one with blue flowers. I found myself thinking about Ellen's green eyes and the adoring way she had looked at me the other day. Nobody had ever looked at me that way before, not even Norma.

Norma and her family were going away skiing for the holidays. They had a place up at Tahoe and generally spent Christmas there.

"I wish you could come too, Jeff."

"I'd like to, Norma, but I always spend Christmas at home. And this year, especially . . ."

"Well, come and have dinner tomorrow night. I'll cook, so it shouldn't be too painful. We're going to get off early Monday morning."

"I can't. I'm going to a birthday party at Ellen's house. It's her birthday."

Norma was trying not to smile.

"What's so funny?"

"Nothing, nothing, Jeff. Well, come over after. I'll wait up for you."

"I'll try, but I don't know how late it's going to go on."

"Whatever time, I'll wait up."

"I'll try."

Norma said slowly, "Don't you want to come, Jeff? We won't be seeing each other for a couple of weeks."

"Well, sure I want to come."

"Because to tell you the truth, Jeff, something is wrong, and I wish I knew what it was."

"It's nothing, Norma."

"Maybe it's all the problems you're having at home. I guess you're worried about Wanda moving out and how your mother is going to take it. Is that it?"

"Yeah—I guess that's it. I'm sorry. I guess I haven't been much fun lately."

"No, you haven't," she said, "but that's what I'm here for. Just remember that, Jeff. I really care about you, and I want to help."

"Thanks, Norma," I said.

"And you'll come tomorrow night?"

"I'll try," I told her.

ten

Ellen looked horrible on her birthday. She was wearing a shapeless dress with pink and white checks and a ruffly collar around her fat neck. Her eyes glittered when she opened the door and saw me standing there.

"Happy birthday, Ellen," I said and handed her the package.

I followed her into the living room where her family was seated, almost as if they had been arranged there, waiting for me. It must have been the event of the year—the arrival of a friend for Ellen. I could see the amazement in her father's face when he saw me. But he controlled himself, shook my hand, and said something friendly.

Mrs. De Luca hurried back and forth from the kitchen to the living room, carrying one tray after another of elaborate hors d'oeuvres. Even though it was Ellen's birthday, it was obvious who the real guest of honor was.

"Well, Jeff, what are you planning on doing after you graduate?" her father asked. He was a small, thin man who spoke with a slight lisp. Later, I found out that he was an accountant.

"I'm still waiting to hear from the schools I applied to."

"Which ones did you apply to?"

"Oh, Berkeley, Stanford . . . I won't get into Stanford, and I guess I won't get into Berkeley either. They'll probably redirect me to Irvine or Riverside. I wouldn't mind San Diego if I can get in there."

"What are you interested in?"

"I wish I knew," I told him.

Everybody laughed. I was the focus of all conversation during the whole evening. Even Ellen's two brothers seemed absorbed in everything I said. I liked it. I found myself speaking with authority on every subject that came up, and being listened to with respect. I advised Matt on the best kind of shoes to wear for soccer, even though I had played it badly as a sophomore. Ricky and

I exchanged stories of how many cars we had dodged on our skateboards, and Mr. De Luca and I disagreed in a friendly, lively way on politics. I sparkled as I felt their admiring glances on me. I couldn't do anything wrong.

Nobody noticed Ellen very much, and she said very little. But her face glowed and she smiled and laughed whenever the others did. Her mother kept pushing food on me. It was a good dinner too—paella and a big guacamole salad. I knew I'd be eating it again later that week, after my mother heard about Ellen's birthday dinner and had to make the same thing, only better.

The only bad moment, and it was a short one, came when I mentioned Norma. I had been telling them about the ceramics class and how frustrated I felt because the clay eluded me.

"Jeff is one of the best," Ellen cried out.

"No, no, no!" I protested. "I'm just a beginner but my girlfriend, she's really exceptional."

All those smiling faces froze just for a very quick second. Then Mrs. De Luca spoke. Passing me the French bread, she asked casually, "Ah, does she expect to do it professionally?"

"Yes, she does. I think her work is good enough right now, but she's planning to go away to Alfred University next year. I'm sure she'll get in. That's one of the best places in the country."

"Where is it?" asked Mrs. De Luca.

"New York state somewhere. I think near Buffalo."

Mrs. De Luca smiled a little more cheerfully and poured some red wine for me.

"I went over to Ida O'Neill's today," said Ellen. "Today I took my first lesson."

She was leaning forward, looking at me, speaking quickly, eagerly.

The wine was warming my cheeks. I felt pleased and very proud that Ellen had acted so quickly on my advice. "That's great!" I said, giving her a big smile of approval.

"She's real nice," Ellen said. "She showed me how to hold my hands, and I didn't have any trouble centering a pot. If I want to, I can come in other days during the week, too, for more lessons."

"Well, Ellen, I can take you over whenever you like," said her mother, trying to sound casual.

Ellen's mother had baked a large German chocolate cake. She carried it into the dining room with seventeen candles burning, and we all sang happy birthday to Ellen.

"Make a wish, dear," her mother urged.

Ellen closed her eyes for a second but I could see the

wish printed on her forehead—*JEFF*. She loomed up over the cake, her huge face serious as she puckered up her mouth. You could hear the blast of air as it snuffed out all the candles.

"Now you'll certainly get your wish," said her mother, being very careful not to look at me.

The cake tasted great. Even my mother would have had a hard time matching it. But Ellen took a little taste and then put her fork back on her plate.

"What's the matter, dear? Isn't it good?" asked her mother.

"It's very good," Ellen said.

"She can eat a whole cake," Ricky told me. "Last year she ate a whole cake. My mother made two, and she ate one all by herself."

There was pride in his voice, the way you would speak if you had an Olympic gold medal winner in your family. But the others all started talking at the same time. Ellen looked at me, her face purpling and tears welling up in her eyes. She shook her head slightly and got up and left the table.

"How about some more cake, Jeff?" her mother asked quickly.

"I'd like another piece," I said heartily.

"I think I'll have another one too, dear, while you're at it." Her father laughed.

There was a lot of movement, dishes clattering, voices raised, laughter. Ellen returned to the table and sat over her plate with the uneaten cake as the rest of us ate and talked and laughed. After a while, she began laughing too.

"Aren't you going to open your presents, Ellen?" asked her mother.

Ellen saved my present for last. First she opened Ricky's. His, Matt's, and her parents' were all wrapped in the same flowery kind of wrapping paper, so I figured that her mother had bought and wrapped all of them. Ricky's present was a pair of fuzzy blue bedroom slippers.

"Oh, thank you, Ricky," Ellen said and rose from her chair, lumbered over to Ricky and kissed him.

"Happy birthday, Ellen," Ricky mumbled.

Matt's gift was a jade heart on a gold chain.

"Oh, isn't it pretty!" Ellen said and barreled over toward Matt, kissing him also.

"Happy birthday, Ellen," Matt said, looking away.

Her parents gave her a hair dryer, and she thanked them and kissed them too.

Then she opened my present. "Oh!" she squealed,

just as if she were a normal, pretty girl. "Oh, it's beautiful, Jeff! I love it!"

"Just the right color for her," said Mrs. De Luca, and the others all murmured their approval as well.

Ellen was looking at me. I knew she wanted to get up and kiss me too as she had the others. I wouldn't have minded, but she didn't.

"Happy birthday, Ellen," I said.

Later, all of them seemed to disappear when we returned to the living room. Somebody must have given a signal, because suddenly Ellen and I were all alone. She had my scarf tied around her neck.

"Good dinner, Ellen. Your folks are really nice."

"I'm glad you came, Jeff."

"Well, I'm glad too."

"And I think the scarf is really beautiful."

"I'm glad you like it."

"It's the most beautiful scarf I ever saw."

"That's nice."

We were sitting on the couch together and I had my arm stretched along the top of it. Every so often while we talked, her body would brush up against my arm.

"You know something?" she said.

"What?"

"I lost two pounds since we had pizza on Tuesday."

"Well, that's great."

"You know how you said I had to lose weight? You know how you said things would be better for me if I did? Well, I think you're right, Jeff. I'm going to try."

So that was why she hadn't eaten any cake that night. Even though she could have knocked the whole cake off, as Ricky said. She was trying to lose weight to please me. I looked into the adoring face of the fat girl sitting next to me and I thought, *She's going to be all right. Because of me. She's going to be all right.* I began patting her shoulder.

"What are you going to do after you graduate, Ellen?" I asked her.

She seemed startled. "I don't know. I never . . . never thought that far ahead."

She didn't say why, but I knew. Because she had been planning to kill herself. But not anymore. Because of me.

"Are you going to college?" I asked her briskly.

"I don't know."

"How are your marks?"

"Okay, I guess. About a B."

"Well, did you apply to any schools?"

"No, I didn't."

"It's not too late. You can still apply to State, and I understand some of the University of California campuses will accept late applications."

Her eyes were on my face. She was listening to what I said, accepting my advice. She was going to live.

"I think you should apply, Ellen."

"Well," she said slowly, "maybe I will. But where?"

"Start with State. Then phone Berkeley and ask about late applications. If you don't get in there, maybe Santa Cruz would take you, or Irvine . . ."

She nodded as I went on talking. Her eyes moved all over my face, but I pretended not to notice.

I arrived at Norma's house about ten thirty. The family were all deep into their packing for the trip to Tahoe. One of Joey's skis was missing, and Mr. Jenkins was shouting, "How can you lose one ski? Answer me that." Mrs. Jenkins was piling jars of fruit compote into cardboard boxes and listening to a recording of *Aida.*

"How come you never can spaghetti sauce or chili?" Lucia demanded. "I'm tired of eating fruit compote all the time. Most of my friends never eat fruit compote. They eat spaghetti or chili."

Nobody noticed me particularly, as usual. Even Norma

was busy up in her room, rolling some of her pots up in rags.

"What are you doing that for?" I asked her.

"A geologist at Berkeley said there might be an earthquake during the next few weeks. I thought I'd better protect some of my pots."

It was funny, but now that Norma wasn't interested in Ellen, I wanted to talk about her. I was high on Ellen.

"I had a very nice time at Ellen's house," I told her.

"Oh, that's right. You went to Ellen's. Here, Jeff, would you just hold this vase up straight for a second?"

"She lost two pounds this week."

"That's nice. Jeff, could you reach up and take down that blue and white bowl from the shelf. I think I'd better wrap that one up too."

"I think she's in love with me, Norma."

"Poor thing!" Norma pushed all of her wrapped pots under her bed. "If anything falls, they'll be protected here," she said.

"I don't think it's such a terrible thing," I said. "She's not talking about killing herself anymore, and I got her to take lessons with Ida O'Neill. And another thing, she's going to register for college. Because I said she should. She'll do anything I tell her."

"Poor thing!" Norma said again. She was still sitting on the floor, looking up at me. Her hair lay rumpled but shiny gold on her head. How beautiful her face was, with its bright blue eyes and sharp clear features. What a contrast to Ellen's.

"Why do you keep saying, 'Poor thing'?" I asked.

"Because if she's in love with you, it's sad."

"Well, I can still be her friend, can't I? I can still help her feel good about herself, and maybe I can get her out of her shell."

Norma shrugged her shoulders. "I just want to wrap up that big pitcher downstairs in the dining room and the long-necked vase in my parents' room, Jeff, and then I'll be finished. Oh, wait! Maybe I'd better do the three green plates, too, and that big blue and white platter . . ."

Norma liked me a lot, I guess, but her pots always came first.

eleven

The one thing my mother did right during the Christmas holiday break was to tell me about Lady Bountiful.

"One of my patients who's very fat has a marvelous robe—all rich golds and oranges. I never saw anything like it. She was the one who told me that she bought it in this special shop, just for fat women. You should tell your friend about it."

Everything else my mother did was wrong. She didn't leave Wanda alone for a minute, nagging at her, carping at her, bugging her over nothing.

I tried to stop her. I still hoped Wanda might change her mind, if my mother could only get off her back.

"Mom," I told her, "Wanda's only fourteen. She's a good kid, but she's only fourteen."

"She's a slob," said my mother. "Did you see the bathroom floor this morning? It's like there's a flood."

"Please, Mom," I said, "just try not to notice. Let's all have a good time this Christmas. Okay, Mom? Let's plan some fun things together. Just the three of us. What do you say?"

My mother bought tickets to the *Nutcracker* ballet. When we were little, she used to take us every year even though I hated it. I still hated it, and Wanda couldn't see anything because there were three tall people sitting in front of us.

I took Ellen over to Lady Bountiful, and as soon as we walked into the store, a saleswoman nearly as fat as Ellen stepped forward and greeted us enthusiastically. She was wearing a long, flowing robe with brilliant splashes of reds and golds. Her eyes traveled over Ellen admiringly.

"What can I do for you?" she asked.

Ellen looked at me, and I said, "Well, we were wondering if you had anything in her size."

The woman's teeth shone as she lead us over to a rack of clothes and began pulling out one dress after another.

"But they're so bright," Ellen protested.

"Yes, they are, honey," said the saleswoman. "Don't you like bright colors?"

"It's not that," said Ellen, "I just thought . . ."

"You thought," the saleswoman said, "that because you were fat you had to wear dark, quiet colors. That you were supposed to wear unobtrusive colors so that nobody would notice you. Well, we don't believe that here. We believe you should wear the most beautiful clothes there are, so that everybody will not only notice you but admire you as well."

She went on talking all the time Ellen was trying on the clothes.

"There's nothing wrong with being fat," she said. "The only thing wrong is listening to people who say it's wrong. Here, honey, I want you to try this purple and green caftan. It will look good with your green eyes."

You could hardly notice Ellen's eyes when she wore the caftan. The brilliant fabric was overpowering and her face seemed lost on top of that mass of color.

"Hmm," said the saleswoman, "you need a little

more makeup and you really have to do something with your hair."

"My hair?" Ellen was cringing before the mirror. "What's the matter with my hair?"

"It's too tame. Let it grow out and wear a big Afro."

"But I don't like curly hair."

"And maybe you need to wear some heavy jewelry. Do you have any of those big clay beads?"

"No, I like pearls."

The saleswoman and I began talking. "They sell a lot of those big necklaces down at Cost Plus," I told her. "And you can get some heavy metal chains there too. I went there a couple of times with my . . . with a friend of mine."

"That's the idea. See, she has to make herself up much bolder. She needs eye makeup and bright red lipstick."

"But my mother doesn't think . . ." Ellen began to say.

"I see what you mean," I said to the saleswoman. "She's really tall enough to carry it, isn't she?"

"Absolutely," said the saleswoman. "She must be about five seven."

"I'm only five six."

"And her hair is too flat on her head. She's got to let

it grow out and wear a big Afro. Here, I'll show you. Sit down over here, honey."

In spite of Ellen's protests, the saleswoman began combing Ellen's hair until it stood out straight around her head. "Actually, she's got quite a bit of body in her hair but she's been wearing it all wrong. She needs a perm."

"My parents just gave me a new hair dryer for my birthday."

"Throw it out," said the saleswoman. "You don't need one with an Afro."

"Well, where should she go for a permanent?" I asked.

"Try Scissors and Shears on California."

"And what about makeup?"

"I hate makeup," Ellen was saying. "It ruins your skin and . . ."

"You can buy some mascara in the dime store and some eye shadow—maybe a green or blue shade for her, and a nice, bright lipstick. She can even smear a little on her cheeks—she has to experiment. But she has a pretty face, so she's off to a flying start."

Both of us paused to inspect Ellen's face in the mirror. She was watching me in the mirror, waiting for me to say whether or not she had a pretty face. Waiting for me to tell her.

"She's going to have a beautiful face," I said, "by the time we're through."

Those two weeks of Christmas were the happiest I had ever spent in my whole life. I managed to stop thinking about my mother and Wanda. When I wasn't working at the hardware store, I was busy with Ellen. I was turning her into a human being.

She completely absorbed me. I started reading fashion magazines—Glamour, Vogue . . . I looked at the painted faces of the models and I learned what to do with Ellen. Money was no problem. Her family was overjoyed to spend it. We bought two caftans at Lady Bountiful and three tunics with matching pants. All of them glowed with brilliant colors and flowed around her body as if she were a monument. There was a gleaming, golden robe that I wanted her to buy, but this time the saleswoman talked me out of it. "Unless she has something really fancy to go to—a formal affair, she wouldn't get much use out of it."

I took her to Scissors and Shears. She went in with her limp hair hanging shapelessly around her face and emerged with a head full of springy curls. I made her buy makeup, and I spent hours with her up in her room, applying lipstick, mascara, and eye shadow.

"Look how it brings out the green in your eyes."

"But it feels funny."

"You'll get used to it. Now, let's try a little of this eyeliner."

We went to Cost Plus and bought heavy bead necklaces and chains with huge metal pendants. She clanked when she walked and I forced her to stand up straight and take long, leisurely steps.

New Year's Eve I spent with her. First, we had dinner at her house and she wore her long, blue caftan with the orange and wine birds-of-paradise design. She had large, golden hoops in her ears, and around her neck hung three strands of red and orange clay beads. I checked her over carefully when she opened the door.

"What kind of shoes are you wearing?"

"My sandals."

"That's good. Now let's take a look at your face."

She turned it up to me and waited for the verdict. "You could have used a little more mascara, but that blue eye shadow is just right. And I like your lipstick. That's a good shade for the dress."

"That's the one you told me to use," she answered.

Ellen's brothers were off with their friends, so we had dinner with only her parents. Ellen ate practically nothing, even though her mother had made stuffed breast of veal. She swallowed a tiny piece of the meat and then slowly ate a small salad without dressing. Whenever she looked at me, I nodded approvingly.

"I do think, Ellen, you could make an exception, since this is New Year's Eve," said her mother in a cranky voice.

"I've lost eight pounds," Ellen said reverently.

"Well, you do have to be careful, dear. You don't want to overdo it."

"I want to lose at least another seventy-two," Ellen insisted.

"But not all tonight," said her mother.

Her father laughed. "Go figure out my wife," he said to me. "For years she's been trying to get Ellen to lose weight, and now that she is . . ."

"Oh, I'm not complaining," said Mrs. De Luca. "I think it's wonderful that she has such self-control, but it is New Year's Eve and I do want her to enjoy herself."

"I am enjoying myself," said Ellen.

"And I do think, dear, that you're wearing much too much makeup for a girl your age."

"But Jeff thinks I should."

Mrs. De Luca sighed and cut me a slice of Nesselrode pie. Ellen didn't have any.

Her parents went to a party that night, so we had the house to ourselves. I helped Ellen clear the table and stack the dishes in the dishwasher. Later, we sat in the living room, and I told her that I thought in the next few weeks we should start filling out college applications for her. She looked scared.

"What's the matter, Ellen? I thought you agreed that you were going to college."

"Yes, I know, but . . ."

"But what?"

She had a panicky look on her face.

"What is it?"

"I don't want to go away from you," she cried, and the tears started spilling all over her face. "I don't want to. I can't. I can't go away from you."

It wasn't midnight yet but I put my arms around her, around all of her, and I kissed her soft mouth very gently. Her eyes were smudged from the tears mingling with the mascara, and I blotted them carefully and rocked her in my arms and told her not to cry anymore. I knew that I had brought her back from death and made a human being of her. She belonged to me now and I would never let her go.

Norma called me as soon as she got back from Tahoe.

"It was great," she said. "Joey broke his ankle and

Carmen got the worst case of sunburn you've ever seen, but I managed to ski every day."

"That's nice," I said.

"Just about everybody was up this year. I met John Kingman—you know him, don't you, Jeff? He's in my French class, and I think he was in your civics class last year—he knows you. And Roger and Dolores were up for a few days. They stayed with us, and one day we all went cross-country skiing, and Roger managed to get lost and . . ."

She went on and on, and I didn't stop her. It didn't matter to me what she was saying or even what was going to happen after she stopped. It was as if I'd never really known her or cared for her, as if she was always way off in the distance, like her voice over the telephone.

Finally, she began winding down. "Well, I really had a marvelous time, but . . . guess what?"

"What?" I asked, looking at my watch. I was going over to Ellen's house and we were going to decide what she should wear on her first day back at school. Then, later, we'd sit in her living room alone—her parents always disappeared—and we'd talk and make plans. She'd watch me and wait—her eyes fixed on my face, especially on my mouth. I knew she was waiting for me to kiss her, wondering if I was going to. She was so new at it, scared too I guess, wondering if I was going to, wanting me to, worrying that I wouldn't. But I wasn't going to hurt her or frighten her. So I'd hold her very gently, and we'd kiss like little kids, and she'd lay her head on my shoulder and listen while I talked to her, and both of us were happy.

"I missed you, you big jerk. If it weren't for missing you, I could have stayed there forever. Next year, you've just got to come up, at least for a few days. And how come you didn't write? Just that one lousy Christmas card. I wrote you just about every day."

"I was busy, Norma."

"Oh!" Her voice grew serious. "Is everything all right at home? Did Wanda move out yet?"

"No, no," I said quickly. "I've been working and, Norma, I have to tell you something."

"What is it, Jeff? Something's wrong. I can hear it in your voice."

"No, nothing's wrong, Norma, but I've been spending a lot of time with Ellen."

"Who?"

"Ellen, Ellen De Luca."

"Oh, Ellen De Luca!" She sounded relieved. "That's nice, Jeff." She began laughing. "Look, why don't you come on over right now, and you can tell me what's been happening with you. The house is a mess and we're eating pickled cauliflower, but you're used to that. Just come on over."

"I can't, Norma, that's what I want to tell you. I can't because I'm going over to Ellen's. I've gotten to really care about her, Norma. I'm sorry, but I'll be going around with her now, and I guess that means it's all over with you and me."

That was how I told her. That was the way I said goodbye to Norma. She didn't deserve it, I know. I should have let her off more gently. She was—she is—one of the nicest girls I ever met. If it weren't for Ellen, who knows, Norma and I might have ended up married one day with a bunch of gorgeous kids and a houseful of gorgeous pots to go with them.

Norma didn't argue with me. She didn't cry, and she didn't say I must have gone off my rocker. She just said, very softly, "Good luck, Jeff," and she hung up.

twelve

I coached Ellen the night before school started. I made her try on different clothes and practice entering the living room over and over again.

"No! No! No!" I told her. "Get your head up and your chest out. Don't cower. People want to slug you when you slump over like that."

She tried. She wanted to please me. In the beginning, that was all she wanted to do.

"Try it again. And this time, don't bump into anything."

Monday morning, I sat in the ceramics class and

waited for her to arrive. As usual, she was late, and the bell had already rung when she appeared in the doorway.

She was wearing a wine-colored caftan with jagged slashes of gold. Four strands of huge wooden and copper beads hung around her neck. I had given her careful instructions about the kind of makeup I wanted her to wear—green eye shadow and a dark, purply red lipstick. Her hair stood out all around her head and large gold earrings hung down almost to her shoulders.

She didn't bump into anything as she moved slowly into the room. But once inside, she suddenly froze. I stirred noisily in my seat. She heard me and directed a pleading, terrified look at me. I smiled and nodded at her and then inclined my head in the direction of her usual seat. She began moving towards it. I looked around the room to see what effect her appearance had created.

Ms. Holland was staring at her. Somebody was laughing. I whirled around, but it was only two girls who were reading a letter together. I could feel eyes on the back of my head, and when I turned again, Roger Torres and Dolores Kabotie swiftly averted their eyes. I knew Norma had told them.

I purposely avoided looking at Norma. She had said, "Hi, Jeff," to me when I entered the room that morning and then had disappeared into the kiln room. There hadn't been any time for me to be embarrassed. All I could think about was Ellen's entrance.

"What a wonderful dress, Ellen," I heard Ms. Holland say as she moved up closer.

Ellen mumbled something not very clearly. I would have to work with her on speaking up and not keeping her head down the way she was doing.

"It's a shame to wear it here though," Ms. Holland continued. "You'll get clay on it. Here, why don't you put this old apron on. It won't cover all of it, but . . ."

Ellen slipped the apron over her dress and dropped into her seat. The room continued humming with its usual sounds, and I pretended to devote all my attention to a shallow bowl I was glazing.

Later, in the hall, as the two of us walked together, I noticed a few people do double takes when they spotted her. I also heard laughter, and so did Ellen.

"They're laughing at me," she said.

"Straighten up your shoulders," I told her. "You have to develop confidence. And pick up your feet. Don't shuffle."

"I look weird in these clothes—and with all this makeup. Nobody else looks like me."

"That's just it, Ellen. You don't want to look like everybody else, do you?"

She remained silent.

"Look, Ellen, I'm telling you that you look great—better than all those silly little cows. You look like a goddess, like Mother Earth—you heard that woman in the store. You have to feel good about yourself "

"But I don't want to look like this," she said.

"I like the way you look," I told her. "Doesn't it matter to you what I think?"

"Yes," she said, turning her face up to me, her green eyes, under all the eye makeup, overflowing with adoration.

"Fine, then," I said, taking her hand. I wanted everybody to see us. I wanted everybody to know that she was my girl and that I was proud of her.

Her hand felt damp with perspiration. Poor Ellen! All those years, how alone she must have felt! But now she had me to look after her.

Somebody laughed. It came wafting back to us. Somebody who had passed was laughing at my Ellen. I could feel her fingers tightening inside my own. I cursed and turned my head. Who was it?

"Never mind, Jeff," Ellen said. "I don't care anymore. As long as I have you, nothing else really matters."

I spent the afternoon with Ellen and didn't get home until nearly six. It was very quiet in the house.

"Mom . . . Wanda . . ." I called out.

Nobody answered, but I heard a rustling sound in the living room. My mother was sitting on the couch, a newspaper spread out on her lap. She was turning the pages with one hand and holding a martini in the other. Usually by six o'clock my mother was busily springing around the kitchen preparing dinner. I couldn't remember when I had ever seen her sitting down reading a newspaper and drinking a martini at six o'clock in the middle of the week.

"Hi, Mom," I said. "Sorry I'm late but I was busy with a friend."

"That's fine, Jeff," she said, smiling at me. "I didn't know when you'd be home, so I just thought I'd relax until you came." She continued turning the pages.

"Anything interesting in the paper, Mom?"

"Just the usual—rapes, murders, fires, child abuse, and taxes." My mother sipped her drink and kept smiling at me.

"Well . . ."

"Are you hungry, Jeff?"

"No, Mom, not terribly. I had some cookies over at Ellen's house."

"Ellen?"

"Oh, yeah, Mom, Ellen. She's my new girlfriend. I thought I told you."

"No, Jeff, you didn't." My mother kept turning the pages without reading anything. "But that's all right. You're entitled to a little privacy, I guess." My mother took another sip, but her hand trembled and some of the drink spilled onto her dress. She didn't seem to notice because she kept smiling at me.

"Are you all right, Mom?" I asked. "Is something wrong?"

"What should be wrong?"

"I don't know."

My mother sipped her drink and turned another page. The house was very quiet.

"Where's Wanda?" I asked. "Isn't she home yet?"

"She's home," said my mother.

"Is she taking a shower?"

"I don't know," said my mother.

"Maybe she and I can fix dinner tonight. You look bushed. You must have had a lousy day."

"I did," said my mother. "But it's not the first."

I stood up. "Just lie down and rest, Mom. Wanda and I will make dinner."

"She's not here."

"What do you mean?"

"Wanda," said my mother. "She's not here."

"I thought you said she was home."

"I did," said my mother, "but this isn't her home anymore. Here! She left this."

My mother handed me a paper. It was a note from Wanda which said:

Dear Mom,

I've been trying to tell you for days but I just couldn't. It's easier to write. I'm going to live with Dad. I just took a small suitcase but I'll come for the rest of my things over the weekend. It doesn't have anything to do with the fight we had last night when you said I was a slob. I've been wanting to go for months. Ask Jeff. He knows and he told me to wait until after Christmas. I think you'll be happier without me but we can still do things together. I love you, Mom, but it's better this way.

Your loving daughter,
Wanda

"I didn't know if you were leaving too," said my mother almost gaily. "That's why I decided to wait for dinner."

"Come on, Mom," I said. "You know I'd never go to live with Dad."

"No," she said, "I don't know. I didn't know Wanda wanted to go either. I guess you knew, but I didn't."

It was horrible the way she kept smiling. "Look, Mom," I said, "she told me before Christmas and I told her to wait. I thought maybe she'd get over it. Maybe she'd just forget it. She didn't say anything during the holidays. I was hoping it would blow over."

"Maybe," said my mother pleasantly, "if you had told me, I might have been able to handle it."

"I tried to warn you, Mom. I kept telling you not to fight with her, not to pick on her."

"I never picked on her," said my mother mildly.

"No . . . no . . . Mom, I didn't mean that."

"I tried to correct her for her own good. She has to learn how to take care of herself."

"Of course she does, Mom, and maybe she'll change her mind. You know Wanda. She's always changing her mind."

"No," said my mother. "She won't change her mind."

She shrugged her shoulders and stood up. "I'll make dinner now, Jeff. What would you like?"

"I don't care, Mom. Anything you want to make is fine with me."

"I was going to make tamale pie tonight because Wanda likes it so much, but maybe I'll make something else. What would you like, Jeff?"

"Anything, Mom. I don't care."

"Well, how about some broiled lamb chops? I know you like lamb chops and I have some in the freezer."

"That sounds great, Mom. Come on, I'll give you a hand."

"No, Jeff, don't bother. I'm sure you've got other things to do. Just go about your business, and I'll call you when dinner is ready."

It was unreal. The two of us kept laughing and chattering while we ate. We didn't leave any quiet, empty spots, and we didn't mention Wanda at all. I told her about Ellen and Lady Bountiful.

"So you've become a fashion designer, Jeff," laughed my mother.

"But I only have one customer," I said, grinning.

"So when do I meet her?"

"Anytime you like, Mom. How about this weekend?"

"Fine, Jeff. Anytime you say."

"But you'll have to make something low in calories. She's on a diet, and she's lost nearly fifteen pounds. She has about seventy more to go."

"She must be quite a handful," giggled my mother, and I burst out laughing. We couldn't stop ourselves after that and kept laughing and laughing hysterically until the phone rang. My mother stopped laughing then.

"I'll answer it, Mom."

"No, Jeff, I can answer it."

My mother arranged her face in a smile, even before she heard who it was. "Why . . . Wanda . . . how is everything working out? . . . That's good . . . That's good . . . Yes . . . Yes . . . Yes . . . I do understand . . . Yes, I do . . . That's all right . . . Yes, of course . . . Yes . . . Yes . . . Whatever you say, Wanda . . . No, I'm fine . . . If that's what you want . . . Yes . . . Saturday is fine . . . Yes, I'll be home . . . Thank you for calling . . . Here he is."

My mother handed me the phone and left the room. Wanda said, "Jeff?"

"Yes."

"Is she still in the room?"

"No."

Wanda let out a deep breath. "Whew, I'm glad that's over! But it wasn't so bad, was it?"

"I don't know what you mean."

"I mean, Mom. She's really taking it great. I thought she'd carry on."

"Listen, Wanda," I said, "she's just putting on a big act. It's killing her."

"No, it isn't," said Wanda. "I know her as well as you do. She's probably glad I've gone. I told her we can get together lots of times, and she said . . ."

"I heard what she said."

"Well, I'm coming over on Saturday to get my things. Will you be home?"

"No, I'm working this Saturday."

"Oh—that's right. I forgot. Well, Dad will be waiting outside for me, so I won't have to stay too long. I'll just pack my clothes. Actually, I got them ready, and I don't have to take everything."

"Wanda," I said, "don't you want to spend a little time with her? Don't you care how she feels?"

It was quiet on the other end. I could hear the kids' voices in the background.

"Wanda?" I said. "Are you there, Wanda?"

"Sure, I'm here," she said, "and stop trying to make

me feel bad. I'm feeling great—it was so much fun eating dinner here tonight. Linda and I made sloppy joes, and Dad's going to take us all out to Farrell's for ice cream."

"Wanda!"

"Here, Dad wants to talk to you, Jeff. 'Bye! See you soon, goon."

My father began talking—explaining—before I even said anything. "Listen, Jeff, I didn't know Wanda was going to leave like that. I kept telling her to talk it over with your mother, and she said she would. So it wasn't my idea."

I could hear Wanda talking to him in the background, telling him it was all right, that Mom had sounded calm.

"It's not all right," I said, but in a low voice. "Wanda doesn't know anything. She should have . . ."

"What's that? Wait a minute, Wanda, I can't hear Jeff."

"I said it was crummy what she did."

"I know, Jeff. I think so too."

Wanda began talking again.

"She's the most selfish, little . . ."

"What's that? Just a minute, Wanda. Look, Jeff, why don't you come over one evening, and we'll be able to talk."

"I can't," I told him. "Especially now."

"I know what you mean. Your mother needs you—that's right. But in a week or so, when it blows over a little bit, come on over and let's talk."

"I'll see."

"We'll talk it over, Jeff—it'll be all right. You'll see. But I don't want you to think it was my idea."

"Okay, Dad, okay."

"Because I told her . . ."

Wanda started talking again.

"Look, Dad, I've got to go now."

"Just a minute. Just a minute! Please, Wanda, just stop talking for a minute."

"I've got to go."

"Why don't you call me, Jeff? Maybe from a pay phone."

"I don't know, Dad. What's the point?"

"I want to talk to you. Maybe I can meet you somewhere. I don't think you really understand."

"Okay, Dad, I'll call."

"I'm working the late shift next week so call me before Monday."

"Okay, Dad, good night."

"Good night, Jeff, and don't forget I'll be waiting to hear from you."

My mother came back into the kitchen after I finished talking. Even though she didn't want me to, I helped her with the dishes. Later, we sat and watched TV together, and when it was time to go to bed, I gave her a kiss. Ordinarily, we're not a kissing family.

"What's that for, Jeff?" she said.

"Oh, nothing special," I said, trying to laugh.

"You're a good boy, Jeff," she said softly, "but I want you to stop worrying about me. Wanda is old enough to make up her mind, and if she wants to go and live with her father, I'm old enough to accept it."

"That's right, Mom."

"So let's just get things back to normal. You don't have to cater to me, and you don't have to change your life."

"Okay, Mom."

"Now let's get to bed and get a good night's sleep."

Which is what I did. Maybe, I figured, Wanda was right. Maybe my mother would be better off without her.

thirteen

I told Ellen I was planning to drop ceramics for the spring semester.

"But why, Jeff?" she asked. "Your pots are really beautiful."

"No, they're not," I told her. "And besides, I've lost interest. I'm just going to spend my last term in high school floating. I only have to take one class in chemistry, one in American history, and maybe I'll take a tennis class and that's it."

"I have to take American history too," Ellen said. "Maybe we can be in the same section."

"Okay. And what else do you have to take?"

"Just another English class and another French."

"And what about P.E.?"

She made a face. "I always got off because I was so fat. The doctor gave me a note saying I didn't have to."

"But I want you to take P.E."

"No, Jeff," she said. "I can't put on shorts. Please, Jeff, don't make me."

I kissed her mouth and ran my hand through her curly, springy hair. But she put an arm on my hand and pleaded, "Please, Jeff, don't make me."

"You need it, Ellen. Your body doesn't have enough muscle tone," I explained. "Especially now that you're losing all this weight. Your skin's just going to hang if you don't do exercise. Let's see—what about swimming?"

"Please, Jeff, I just couldn't get into a bathing suit. Not yet, Jeff. Don't make me!"

I patted her soft shoulder and said, "Okay, Ellen, don't get upset. You know I'm not going to make you do anything that's not good for you. Hmm—how about tennis?"

"Please, Jeff!"

"Okay, well that leaves gymnastics or maybe jazz dancing. They've just started giving courses in jazz dancing, and

I think you can wear your clothes, but you will get a good workout."

"Do I have to, Jeff?"

"Yes, Ellen, you do. But you know what?"

"What, Jeff?"

"Maybe I'll take it with you."

She looked up at me with her eyes full of love. Of course she agreed. She agreed to everything I told her in the beginning.

Except for ceramics.

"You can drop it too," I said. "There's no reason why you should keep taking it either."

She was wearing a purple tunic over a purple pair of pants that day. The neckline was a deep V, and I liked the way the purple contrasted with her white skin. She was watching me, solemnly. "Do I have to?" she said.

"Have to what?"

"Have to drop ceramics?"

"Don't you want to?"

She shook her head, and hundreds of fat little curls swished in the air. "No, I like it. Ida O'Neill says it's a good idea to work every day if I really want to improve. She thinks I should stay in the class, even if Ms. Holland isn't such a good teacher."

"Well, you don't have to study with Ida O'Neill either. Why don't you just drop the whole thing? I only suggested it originally because I didn't think you had enough interests. But now that you do, you don't need it."

Ellen thought for a moment. "Interests? Like what?"

"Well," I explained, "you've got me, haven't you? And you'll take jazz dancing, and I think I'm going to take you to a few basketball games . . . We'll see . . . We'll talk about other interests as we go along."

"But I like ceramics," Ellen said. "Don't you think I've improved?"

One of her pots, a little, tubby, shiny pink one was sitting on the kitchen table with a fat, little cactus plant inside it. We were sitting there, me munching cookies and drinking milk, and Ellen slowly sipping a diet soda. Other tubby pots with shiny glazes had been distributed throughout the house, mostly in the bathrooms, by her tactful mother.

"Of course," I said indulgently, "and if you really are enjoying it, Ellen . . ."

"Oh I am, I am," she said.

"Well then, why don't you just go right on."

"Thanks, Jeff," she said.

I was bringing Ellen home for dinner that Saturday

night. We spent Friday night together, and I kept reassuring her that my mother would like her. It was late when I returned home that night, and my mother had gone to bed. There was a note from her telling me not to eat the cheese pie in the refrigerator, that it was a low-calorie one she was planning to serve for dessert on Saturday night when Ellen came for dinner.

Saturday morning, Wanda was coming over at about ten to pick up her things. I had to leave the house at eight thirty to be at the hardware store by nine. My mother was still asleep, which was surprising. Usually she gets up early every day, even on weekends when she doesn't normally work. I tiptoed around the house, and carefully closed the door when I left for work.

My father was waiting for me in the hardware store when I returned from lunch at one o'clock.

"Jeff," he said, "can you come outside? I need to talk to you."

I followed him outside the door. Wanda, I figured, it had to be Wanda. His face looked grim. She was giving him a hard time. Good, I thought. Now he's getting a taste of her moods and bad temper.

"I'm very sorry to tell you this, Jeff," said my father, "but when Wanda and I got to your house . . . Well, Jeff, it's okay now . . . she's going to be okay . . . But your mother, we found your mother . . . She . . . she'd taken sleeping pills . . . She tried to commit suicide."

I must have staggered, because he put his arms around me. I could smell his sweat, and I remembered how I used to smell it when I was a little boy and he'd held me in his arms.

"It's all right, Jeff. Why don't you take off the rest of the day? I've got my car here and we can go back to my house. Wanda's there. She's been pretty upset, but she'll feel better when she sees you."

"Where's Mom?" I said.

"At the hospital. She's all right now, Jeff. The doctor said . . ."

"I want to see her."

"Okay, Jeff, I'll take you there. They'll keep her there a week or so until the doctors feel she won't do it again. I don't know if she'll even be awake now, but I guess you can see her."

She was awake—barely, lying there, small and dark, with a smile on her face.

"Why did you do it, Mom?" I said, trying not to cry. My father was waiting for me outside in the waiting room. I took her hand. It felt cold. "Why, Mom, why?"

Her hand began patting mine. She didn't say anything. She just smiled and patted my hand.

"Just because that little bitch, Wanda, went away? Is that why, Mom?"

"No," she whispered finally. "No . . . maybe . . . yes . . . but it wasn't your fault, Jeff . . . Don't feel bad . . . You're a good boy . . . Don't feel bad."

The nurse made me leave, but I told my mother I'd be back the next day.

"Pick up some things," said my father, "and we'll go to my place. You'll stay with us while she's in the hospital. Later when she comes out, if she comes out, I'm not sure, Jeff, but maybe you'd better plan on staying with us."

"No," I told him. "I'm not staying with you. And I don't want to see Wanda. It's her fault. If it weren't for her, Mom never would have done it."

"Don't say that, Jeff," my father said, putting his arm around me as we walked out of the hospital. But I pulled away this time. "Jeff! Jeff!" said my father. "She's a very unhappy woman. She always was. Nobody can change that—not even you. And you know—I don't want to criticize her—but for a mother to lay this kind of trip on her own child! Do you know what Wanda's going through now?"

"I don't care what Wanda's going through," I shouted at my father, "and I don't want to see her. Just take me back home—my home! That's where I want to go."

He argued, but he couldn't shake me. We drove around while we argued. Then we ate some pizza and drove around some more. Finally, the two of us came back to my place. I kept telling him he could leave me, but he said no. I didn't want him to know it, but I was afraid to stay by myself and I was glad he stayed over. He slept in Wanda's bed, and at night I woke up shaking with terror for the first time in weeks. I walked past her room and looked inside. He was asleep—my big father in Wanda's small bed. He didn't belong there. He had no right sleeping in my mother's house. It made me angry seeing him there, and I wondered what would happen if he woke up. Would he know I was scared? Would he put his arms around me and tell me it was going to be all right-that everything was going to be all right?

But he didn't wake up. I walked into the kitchen, opened the refrigerator and saw the low-calorie cheese pie wrapped carefully in plastic paper. I had forgotten all about Ellen. I ate half the cheese pie and thought about Ellen. After a while, I calmed down and was able to go back to bed.

My father refused to leave the next day unless I came with him or found someone to stay on at the apartment with me. I called my Aunt Lisa, Mom's younger sister, and told her. She wanted me to come and stay with her and Uncle Roger in Kensington. I refused. My father was talking to me all the time I was talking to my Aunt Lisa. I couldn't hear either one of them. Finally, I handed him the phone, and he and my aunt talked while I wandered around the kitchen. I was hungry and I opened the refrigerator as my father said, "Sure, Lisa, that's right. You understand I don't want to leave him, but he won't come with me. Sure, Lisa, thanks, Lisa . . . I sure appreciate . . ."

There wasn't too much in the refrigerator aside from the half of the low-calorie cheese pie. Ellen! I had to call Ellen. She must have sat around waiting for me the night before, wondering what had happened.

"Okay," my father was saying into the phone, "why don't we meet you over at the hospital?"

"Dad," I said, "I've got to make a call."

"Sure, Lisa . . . in about an hour and a half . . . Sure, Lisa . . . Goodbye." He hung up and began explaining to me what my Aunt Lisa had said to him and what he'd said to her.

"Just a minute, Dad," I told him. "I've got to make an important call."

Ellen answered after one ring. "Hi, Ellen," I said. "Look, I'm sorry I didn't call you yesterday. Something happened—my mother—well, she's in the hospital. She's all right now, but it was kind of tense here, and I'm sorry, Ellen, I just forgot."

"That's all right, Jeff," Ellen said. "I knew you'd call. My mother said—well, never mind what she said. But I knew you'd call."

My father was sitting in the kitchen waiting for me to finish, so he could tell me the arrangements he and my Aunt Lisa had worked out. He was pretending to be looking at a magazine and not listening to me, but I knew he was. I wanted to tell Ellen how much I loved her, and that she'd never have to worry about me standing her up. I felt all choked up at the way she trusted me so completely, but my father was sitting there, pretending to read a magazine. So I just said, "You never have to worry about me, Ellen. I can't talk now, but I'll call you as soon as I can."

"I'll be here, Jeff," she said.

Aunt Lisa met us at the hospital. She was carrying a plant, and she told me she'd stay on with me at the apartment until my mother returned. She and I both went in to see my mother while my father waited outside. My mother was sitting up in bed, her hair combed, her face carefully made up, that little smile still there.

"Lisa!" she said when she saw my aunt. She wrinkled her nose as if something smelled bad.

"Hi, Sue," said my aunt. She kissed my mother, and the two of them smiled carefully at each other.

"Hi, Mom," I said, and waited for somebody to say something.

"Well," said my aunt finally, "I thought I'd never get here. You should have seen the traffic on the bridge."

"It's always like that on Sunday," said my mother.

"But not like today."

"Lisa, have you got an emery board?" my mother asked. "One of my nails broke this morning."

Neither of them said anything about my mother's suicide attempt. My mother asked after Uncle Roger, as if she'd just seen him, and my aunt told a couple of funny stories about some of the customers in her sporting goods store.

"How about a milk shake, Sue? I bet the food here's atrocious."

"I'm used to hospital food," said my mother, "but my throat is awfully dry."

"Well, I'll just run down to the coffee shop. What about you, Jeff? Would you like a milk shake too?"

"No thanks, Aunt Lisa."

"Soda?"

"Nothing thanks. But why don't I go and get it?"

"No, no, no! It's my treat."

"She doesn't want to be alone with me," said my mother after Aunt Lisa had gone. "She's embarrassed."

"Oh, I don't know, Mom."

"She'd never do anything so crude—not her—with her fancy house, her doting husband, and all her money. She never even had kids because she probably thought it was vulgar."

"Mom, Mom . . ."

"Whose idea was it to call her?" my mother snapped. "I bet it was your father's."

She wasn't smiling anymore. Maybe it was just as well. Maybe things finally were going to get back to normal.

fourteen

My mother remained in the hospital for a week. I went to see her every day, and so did my Aunt Lisa. We went at different times. I don't think she complained to my aunt about me. Maybe she did. I don't know. But she certainly complained to me all the time about her.

"She always had all the breaks," my mother said. "Life's been easy for her."

"I don't know how you can say that," I told her. "First of all, you know she had polio when she was a child, and she still has a pretty bad limp."

"Big deal!" said my mother. "Everybody was always sorry for her, because they thought she was so helpless.

She got all my mother's attention, and everybody in the family always said 'poor dear,' and 'wasn't she something to manage in spite of her handicap.' Bull! It was because of her handicap that she got all the breaks."

"Well, she really cares for you, Mom, and she's been wonderful. So has Uncle Roger. You know how hard it is for him to manage without her at the store, but he says she should stay on here as long as we need her."

"I don't need her, and I don't want her pity either, you hear me, Jeff? I want her out of the house when I get home."

"Mom, Mom . . ."

"And how come Wanda hasn't been to see me? She sent me one lousy get well card and that's it."

"I don't know, Mom, but I'll call her when I get home."

I hadn't spoken to Wanda since the Saturday my mother tried to kill herself, but my father called me at least once every day. I told him that Mom wanted to see Wanda, and that shut him up for a change.

"Dad?"

"I know, Jeff, but I don't think it's a good idea."

"Why not?"

"Well, you know Wanda's been taking it pretty hard.

She's been going for counseling, and I think maybe for the time being . . . until she feels a little better . . ."

"Look, Dad, Mom's the one who's in trouble. Let me talk to Wanda."

"No, Jeff, not if you're going to make her feel bad. She's been through enough."

My father was only worried about Wanda. All he could think of was how Wanda was suffering. Didn't he care how I was suffering? Here I was hanging on to the phone trying not to break down and start bawling. Nothing I said made any difference at all to him. Wanda was the one he liked better—the one he fussed over the most. And now she was living with him and going out to Farrell's for ice cream and crying on his shoulder and smelling his warm, sweaty, comforting smell.

"Jeff?"

It was like my mother and Aunt Lisa. The way my mother felt about Aunt Lisa, Wanda always had all the breaks too. Even my mother—she must have loved Wanda the best too, if she needed to kill herself just because Wanda took off.

"Jeff, are you still there?"

"Yes."

"So I really don't want you to make Wanda feel bad. I know you feel bad too . . ."

"No, you don't," I said. "You don't know anything about me." I hung up and took the phone off the hook.

Aunt Lisa tried, but she wasn't much help either. I was glad she was there at night, when I woke up with the shakes and heard her deep, even breathing coming from my mother's bed. But during the day, I knew that she was an ally of my father and that he'd been coaching her.

"Wanda wants to have dinner with us tonight," said my Aunt Lisa. "I thought we might all go out to that nice little Japanese restaurant on Judah. Maybe Roger can join us and your father too."

"Sorry," I told her. "I have a date with my girlfriend."

"Don't be like that, Jeff," said my aunt. "Don't go blaming Wanda for what happened. If you start blaming, it's hard to know where to stop, Maybe you could blame me, because your mother and I haven't been in touch for over a year. Maybe you could say it was your father's fault, because they were divorced, or your fault, because you weren't home that morning. It can go on and on and never stop."

"I really do have a date with my girlfriend," I said.

That was the only good time for me—when I was

with Ellen, my big, fat, loving, happy Ellen. And she was happy now. Because of me. Maybe I couldn't do anything right with my own family, but with Ellen I couldn't do anything wrong.

She didn't know the truth about my mother. I only told her that my mother had passed out and was undergoing tests in the hospital. She didn't ask me any further questions.

Ellen was going to Weight Watchers now. She had lost twenty pounds and was growing impatient.

"It's slowing down," she complained. "I'm eating even less than I did when I started out, but I'm only losing a few pounds a week now."

"There's no hurry," I told her.

"Yes, there is," she said. "You're forgetting that the prom is May 28th. I want to lose eighty pounds by then. That's only four months away."

Ellen kept talking about the prom. When she first mentioned it to me, I said no. Nothing and nobody was going to get me to go to the prom. She didn't argue, but I could see she was disappointed. Then I began thinking. I began thinking about her in the shiny, gold caftan I'd seen in Lady Bountiful. We could come late to the prom and maybe everybody would be dancing as we began descending the stairs into the main ballroom. I'd coach her, and she'd move slowly, gracefully, magnificently, one step at a time. Maybe she would be wearing some kind of gold ornament in her hair and heavy gold bracelets on her arms. Her face would be radiant with smiles, and when she looked at me with those big, adoring eyes, everybody would be able to see how much I meant to her.

So I told her we could go, and all the lights went on in her face. I told her about the gold caftan. "Like in a fairy tale, Ellen. You'll be all in gold."

"But Jeff," she said, "I won't need to wear a caftan by then because I'm going to be thin."

Thin? I burst out laughing as Ellen looked at me solemnly.

"What's funny, Jeff?" she asked.

"I don't know, Ellen," I told her, patting her soft, fat check. "It's just hard for me to think of you as thin."

"But I will bc, Jeff," she said. "You'll see. I will. I really will."

"It's okay, Ellen," I told her. "I love you just the way you are."

"Do you really, Jeff?" she said, watching my mouth

again. "Do you really love me—I mean, as much as you used to love Norma?"

"Of course, you big silly. Of course I love you as much as I loved Norma. More than I loved Norma. More than I ever loved anybody. I'll never love anybody the way I love you."

The good times with Ellen got better and better. I started sleeping through the night again. I even went over to my father's house and made up with Wanda. She looked smaller than I had remembered. Poor Wanda! I felt sorry for her. Poor Mom! Poor Dad! I was sorry for all of them, because I was safe and very high on Ellen.

My mother came home from the hospital, and Aunt Lisa offered to stay a few more days. My mother said no. She said some other things too, so that my aunt was barely speaking to her by the time she left. I helped her carry her things downstairs to her car, and she hugged me hard before she drove off.

"Don't forget, Jeff. Call me if you need me."

"I will, Aunt Lisa, and thanks for everything."

"Tell your mother I'll give her a ring later." She shook her head. "I guess I'll just have to control myself and not get sore."

"She doesn't mean anything, Aunt Lisa. That's just the way she talks."

She smiled and patted my arm. "I've known her longer than you have, Jeff. Long enough to know she does mean it, but maybe it's better for her when she gets it out in the open."

My mother was upstairs in Wanda's room when I returned. "I think," she said, "that maybe I'll turn this into a sewing room."

Wanda had been over once while my mother was still in the hospital and had collected most of her things. The room had an undressed look to it.

"Of course," my mother went on, "I suppose the smartest thing to do would be to find a smaller apartment. You'll be going off to college in the fall, and I'll only need a one-bedroom place."

"But I'll be back," I protested.

"Weekends, holidays," said my mother. ". . . At first, but after a while . . ."

"Look, Mom, please," I said, "don't do anything right now. Don't change anything. Let's leave everything just the way it is."

"My poor boy," said my mother. "You never did like change, did you?"

She was thinner and her little face had a yellowish hue.

"Depends on the change," I said. "If it's for the better . . ."

"Most change is for the worst," said my mother.

"No, Mom, not always. Take my girlfriend, Ellen. I wish you had seen her before. She never looked you in the eye. She had no confidence. She was always dropping things and bumping into doors. I've been working with her, and now she stands up straight and looks you right in the eye. She feels good about herself now. I've taught her how to dress, and she has confidence."

"I can't wait to meet her," said my mother.

I thought of the low-calorie pie in the refrigerator the night before she tried to kill herself, but I tried to sound cheerful when I said, "How about this Saturday night, Mom? I can bring her over this Saturday, if you like."

"Fine," said my mother. "I'll make something that's not fattening."

My mother and I settled into our old routine. We didn't talk about her suicide attempt, and she went back to work and started seeing a shrink a couple times a week. But nothing seemed to change. She and Wanda began talking to each other over the phone, and my father said that maybe in a couple of weeks, if Wanda felt stronger, she could come over and have dinner.

When I picked Ellen up the night she came to my house for dinner, she showed me how the tunic she was wearing gaped around her neck. I should have been pleased, but I wasn't.

"I've lost twenty-three pounds now," Ellen said, "and all my clothes are beginning to hang on me."

"You're pushing too hard," I told her. "You'll get sick if you're not careful."

"One day," Ellen said dreamily, "I'm going to be thin, really thin. I'm going to wear shorts and a bathing suit . . ."

"I think we should go to Lady Bountiful and buy you some new clothes," I told her.

"No. I don't want any new clothes. I want to just wear these until I can get into some regular clothes. I want to watch how they begin to hang on me. If it gets too bad, my mother can always take them in."

She had a package in her hand, wrapped in fancy paper.

"What have you got there?" I asked.

"It's a present for your mother."

"What kind of present?"

"You'll see." She smiled and looked sly, and I patted her on her shoulder. How happy she was! I felt a glow of pride thinking that only a few months ago, this rosy-faced girl with the sparkling eyes was ready to kill herself. I noticed that her lipstick seemed too pale for her face.

"What's that shade of lipstick you're wearing?" I asked her.

"Oh Jeff, it's a new one—Spring Blush—I just bought it yesterday."

"I don't like it. It's too pale for your skin, and it doesn't go with the purple of your tunic."

She looked guilty. "I just got tired of wearing those same old dark colors all the time."

"Well, we can get you some other ones if you're looking for something new," I told her patiently. "But I'd better go with you. That shade is all wrong."

"Okay, Jeff," she said. "I'll take it off. But which one should I use?"

My mother looked astonished when she saw Ellen. But it didn't bother me. I was proud of the way Ellen stood up straight and looked my mother in the eye and said, "Hello, Mrs. Lyons," in a clear, cheerful voice. She handed my mother the package.

"Oh my," said my mother, "you shouldn't have." She unwrapped it and held in her hand a fat, stubby, shiny pink teapot that only Ellen could have made.

It irritated me, but I kept it to myself for the time being.

"Umm!" said my mother, holding it away from her and pretending to admire it. "It's . . . uh . . . very interesting. Did you make it yourself?"

"Uh huh," said Ellen. "I did, and I worried all week that it wouldn't be fired in time."

"Well, thank you, dear," said my mother. "I know I'm going to enjoy it very much. Maybe we can all have a cup of tea later."

Ellen ate her food very slowly and neatly, while my mother and I did most of the talking. My mother did make tea, and it dripped out of the teapot spout all over the table.

After we left, Ellen didn't want to go home. She asked me to drive her out to the beach.

"The beach?" I said. "Why the beach?"

She mumbled something about a girl in one of her classes who told her that she and her boyfriend often drove out to the beach at night to watch the moonlight on the waves.

"There's no moon out tonight," I said, but I drove out anyway and parked above the ocean among a bunch of other cars. Loud rock music came from the car on our left.

"But there's nobody there," Ellen said, looking through our car window. "Do you think they just forgot to turn off the radio?"

"No," I told her. "They're still inside, only they're making out down on the backseat. That's why you don't see any heads."

"Oh!" she said.

I put an arm around her and began telling her how proud of her I was. I told her that I thought she should keep working on her posture, but that I liked the way she kept her head up while she was speaking to my mother.

"Jeff," she said, looking away from me, "Jeff, did you ever . . ."

"What, Ellen?" I kissed the top of her head.

"I mean—did you ever come out here with . . . with Norma?"

"No," I told her, "not with Norma."

"With . . . with anybody else?"

"Maybe." I laughed. "But don't worry, Ellen, I'm not going to drag you into the backseat. Not you."

"No," she said, "no. I didn't think you would."

Later, as I drove her home, I told her I thought she ought to quit taking lessons with Ida O'Neill.

"You go at least once a week and sometimes even twice or three times," I told her. "It cuts into our time together."

"I won't go so often," she said quickly. "I'll only go once a week from now on."

"What's the point, Ellen?" I said kindly. "You're never going to be really good at it."

She didn't say anything. I was driving her home, and I was feeling calm and happy and very much in love. I reached over and took her hand, and she said, "Jeff!"

"What is it?"

"I don't want to give up ceramics. I like it . . . I love it . . . and I think . . ."

"What do you think?"

"I think I'm going to be good at it someday. I'm getting better all the time. Dolores Kabotie—you're not in the class anymore—but she was looking at a pot I made last week, and she said she thought it was very unusual."

"That doesn't mean she thought it was good."

Suddenly, Ellen was crying. I could hear her big,

heavy sobs. I pulled over and put my arms around her and pulled her wet face against mine.

"What is it, Ellen? What is it?"

"Oh, Jeff," she cried, "don't make me give it up. I love it so much now, and I know I'm going to be good at it. I just know I will, and you'll be proud of me. Please, Jeff!"

I knew she'd never learn to make a decent pot in her life, but what could I do? I loved her, didn't I? I only wanted her to be happy. That was all I ever wanted for her. So I told her she didn't have to stop, and she kept kissing me and kissing me with her wet face full of tears.

fifteen

By the end of March, Wanda was coming over for dinner nearly every Wednesday night. Every so often, she'd spend the weekend as well. She complained all the time to my mother about Linda.

"She's a real slob, Mom. You should see the inside of the stove. It makes you want to throw up. And the shower is so tacky. I wish I didn't have to use it."

"Why do you stay?" I asked her one night as I was driving her home.

"Because I love it," she said.

"But you complain all the time about Linda."

"That's only because I want Mom to feel good.

Linda's the greatest. She never yells at me, and the kids are cuties. Okay, Sean does have a temper and David gets into my things, but they're good kids. And Dad—well . . ." She laughed. "You know Dad."

It hurt me, watching my mother's hope blossoming.

She never did turn Wanda's room into a sewing room. Instead, she bought a new, frilly bedspread for Wanda's bed and some lace curtains for the windows. She was always on good behavior when Wanda came home. I tried to warn her.

"I think Wanda's skin isn't looking too good," said my mother one morning at breakfast.

"Like most other fourteen-year-olds," I said.

"Well," said my mother, "you never had any trouble with your skin. I think it's her diet."

"You're right," I agreed. "She does eat a lot of junk food."

"No," said my mother. "When she lived here, I was pretty careful to see that she didn't. But of course, now . . ."

My mother slowly chewed on a piece of toast and waited for me to answer. I knew she wanted me to say that Wanda wasn't looking good, that she'd look better if she were back with us. She wanted me to say that I thought Wanda might want to come home. I didn't say anything.

"Last time she was here," my mother continued, "she told me that Linda goes in for a lot of starches. Sometimes she even serves rice and potatoes at one meal. Wanda says they're all overweight."

She waited for me to agree.

"Dad is," I said finally, "a little. But Linda and the boys are kind of thin."

"Wanda says they're all overweight."

"Mom," I said carefully, "I think Wanda can take care of herself. You don't have to worry about Wanda. She always lands on her feet."

"I don't know what you're talking about," said my mother between her teeth. "All I said was that Wanda's skin was bad."

"That's right, Mom," I said, getting up quickly and picking up my plate. "I agree, so let's not get into a fight."

Of course we did, and my mother went right on hoping.

By the end of March, I knew that I wanted to marry Ellen. Maybe not right away—we were too young for that. But in the fall, if we both went to the same school, we could start living together. Plenty of kids did nowadays. There shouldn't have been any problem. My mother might have made a fuss, but she'd get over it. And Ellen's family would have agreed to anything I wanted. They were crazy about me. They knew I had transformed their daughter and they came right out and said so, particularly Ellen's mother.

I was sitting with her in the living room one Saturday evening, waiting for Ellen to get back from Ida O'Neill's.

"She won't even let me pick her up anymore—she's getting so independent," her mother said proudly. "She takes the bus everywhere, and soon she'll have her own license."

I looked at my watch. It was six thirty.

"Doesn't she usually get back earlier?"

"Sure she does. Especially if she knows you're picking her up. She doesn't want to lose a minute." She smiled at me. "Are you hungry, Jeff? How about some cheese and crackers?"

"No, thanks, Mrs. De Luca. We're supposed to be having dinner with that friend of hers from Weight Watchers—Nancy Something."

"Nancy Rosenfeld. You haven't met her yet, have you, Jeff?"

"No, but Ellen keeps talking about her."

"Well—she really is a lovely girl—nice figure too.

She lost over eighty pounds and she's been giving Ellen all sorts of tips."

I knew I wasn't going to like Nancy Rosenfeld. Mrs. De Luca kept on talking, and I tried not to be irritated. Ellen was late, and it wasn't the first time. If it wasn't Ida O'Neill, it was Nancy Something, or another friend she'd made at Weight Watchers. I looked at my watch and Mrs. De Luca said, "You know how the buses are—she probably had a long wait."

"I could have picked her up," I said. "I finish work at five, and I could just have gone over and gotten her. We could have gone right from there to meet her friends."

"I guess she wanted to come home first and change. I fixed her wine-colored caftan today. It just hangs on her now. She's lost about thirty-seven pounds."

"I keep telling her to get some new clothes," I said.

Mrs. De Luca laughed. "I know, Jeff. So do I, but she keeps saying she wants to wait until she can wear regular clothes. A few months ago, I never would have believed it possible. Before you took an interest in her, Jeff. She's a different person because of you."

The look in Ellen's mother's eyes was nearly as overpowering as the one in Ellen's eyes.

Ellen arrived home at seven fifteen. She came flying through the door, her cheeks glowing.

"Oh Jeff," she said, "I'm so sorry, but I was waiting for the kiln to be unloaded. I made you something. I wanted to give it to you." She held out an object wrapped in newspaper.

"We're going to be late, Ellen," I said, trying to control my annoyance. "Weren't we supposed to meet them at seven o'clock?"

"Oh, I called Nancy and changed it to eight. I'll hurry and get dressed. But Jeff, aren't you going to look at what I made for you?"

I unwrapped it and found a fat, blotchy cream-colored mug that had JEFF printed on it in crooked orange letters.

"Wonderful!" I told her. "Thanks a lot—and now I think you ought to get ready."

I could hear her bubbling away to her mother, her laughter billowing down the stairs. It should have made me feel happy, but I wasn't looking forward to the evening. I preferred having Ellen all to myself.

The evening was a flop. Nancy kept chattering on and on to Ellen about the people in their Weight Watchers' group. I didn't like her. She was nineteen, a student at

City College, and she wore cheap perfume that made me sick to my stomach. She also kept giving Ellen advice on how to dress.

"You can probably start wearing regular clothes now," she said, "something with a little more shape. You don't have to keep wearing those old sacks. Why don't we go shopping next week?"

"Okay," said Ellen.

"You don't have to buy a lot of things because you're going to keep losing weight, but it will probably take another six months before you get all the way down."

"Oh no!" wailed Ellen. "I wanted to lose it all before my prom."

"When is the prom?" Nancy asked.

"The end of May."

"Well," said the Voice of Experience, "you might lose another fifteen or twenty pounds by then. You'll look nice, but you won't be all the way down."

"She'll look gorgeous," I said, "and for the time being, she can manage with the clothes she has. I think she looks pretty good the way she is."

"I do too," said Nancy's boyfriend. He was a little weasel-faced fellow who worked at McDonald's and had a smell of fried onions about him. He kept eyeing Ellen all through the evening. "She's kind of classy, the way she dresses. Even if she was thinner, she'd look good in those clothes."

I didn't need his support, and by the end of the evening I felt like knocking him down. I didn't like the way he kept looking Ellen over, and the way he always managed to brush up against her. She didn't notice. But I told her later, back at her house. I told her I didn't like Nancy, and I certainly didn't like her boyfriend.

"But why, Jeff?"

"Because she's a big busybody—sticking her nose into everybody else's business. And her boyfriend is a punk. Didn't you see the way he was coming on to you? And Nancy doesn't have any taste at all, with that cheap perfume and her sleazy clothes. When the time comes, I'll go with you to buy new clothes. Okay?"

"Okay, Jeff, but she's such a nice girl, and she's been so good to me."

Ellen was high that night. She kept yakking on and on. She wanted to tell me about the ceramics class at school—about Dolores Kabotie, Roger Torres, and Norma Jenkins.

"Dolores made a wide pot with the most beautiful handles you ever saw. She glazed it all in a shiny black glaze and scratched wonderful swirling designs down at the base."

"That's nice," I said.

"Roger's been working on cobalt glazes. He's kind of secretive."

"I never liked him much," I said.

"Oh, he's okay when you get to know him. Norma says he's just got a mild paranoid streak when it comes to his glazes. Otherwise he's okay. Norma says . . ."

"What's this with 'Norma says'?" I interrupted. "Since when have you and Norma gotten so chummy?"

Ellen laughed. "I guess we are getting kind of friendly. She's a very nice girl."

"I told you that a long time ago," I said, "but I also remember you saying that you hated her."

Ellen said lightly, "I must have been jealous of her then, but not anymore. I think she's just great. She's the best potter in the class, but she's not stuck up about it. Yesterday she showed me how to apply slip to a partially dried pot . . ."

I hardly ever saw Norma anymore. Once in a while, she'd come bounding down the hall, hair flying, arms full of pots. Sometimes I'd lose myself in the crowd. Whenever she saw me, she'd flash a big smile and look as if she'd like to stop and talk, but I always moved on. She was ancient history to me.

Ellen's voice turned worshipful as she continued talking about Norma, Roger, and Dolores. She sounded like me a few months back.

"Ellen," I asked her, "do you ever think about suicide?"

She stopped chattering and took a deep breath. "No," she said, "not anymore."

We were sitting on the couch in her living room. As usual, the rest of her family had evaporated as soon as we appeared. I wanted her to tell me she never thought about suicide anymore because of me.

"It's because of you," Ellen said. She turned her face towards me. Her green eyes seemed to grow bigger and bigger as she continued losing weight. I touched her soft face and felt the happiness inside me deepen.

She lay her head on my shoulder and began to talk. "It was miserable, Jeff. I couldn't escape out of it. I was trapped inside all that fat, and the more my mother talked and the shrink talked and everybody else talked, the worse it got."

Her head felt heavy on my shoulder, but I didn't move.

"I talked about killing myself, and sometimes I liked to think about it when there wasn't anything good on TV. But you know, Jeff, I never would have done it, because I always knew there was going to be another way out for me."

"What do you mean?"

"I mean I knew something was going to happen."

"You mean a knight on a white charger was going to come along and rescue you?"

"Yes—that's what I thought for a while—like in the fairy tales. And you did come along. But it wasn't that either."

Her head was too heavy and I began squirming. She lifted it and smiled at me.

"Well, what was it then?"

"I knew I was going to change. I knew a time would come when I would change. I always knew it deep, deep down. And I think you must have known it too. I think you must have understood that I really wanted to change. You were wonderful to me, Jeff. I'll never forget the way you saw something in me that nobody else saw."

Her eyes glowed with that worshipful light. I took her hand. "I think we're good together, Ellen. I think we're wonderful together. That's what I want to tell you. I want to talk about us—nobody else. I think we should live together. In the fall, I mean, when school starts. We still haven't heard from the schools we applied to, but if we decide to go to the same school, there's no reason why we can't get a place together. I hope it'll be San Diego, but if we don't get in there, we probably will in Santa Cruz or Riverside. Lots of kids live together nowadays."

Ellen hesitated and looked away. "Sure, Jeff," she said finally. "But . . ."

"But what? Are you afraid your mother will make a fuss?"

"No, it's not that."

"So?"

"Well, it's just that I don't know if I really want to go to college now, Jeff. I love ceramics so much. I was thinking maybe I could just stay here and keep on taking lessons from Ida O'Neill for a year or so. I mean, until I'm good."

"But Ellen, I'm not going to be here in the fall."

"Well, I haven't said anything. I mean, I was just thinking, but . . ."

"Well, you can just put it out of your mind. Maybe you can play around a little over the summer, but in the fall you don't want to waste your time. You want to start college and get on with your life. You have a career to think about."

"What kind of a career, Jeff?"

"How should I know?" I said impatiently. "But

something you're good at. After you start school, you'll take different courses, and you'll find something that you like. It's going to be the same for me. I don't know what I want either. But I do know I want the two of us to be together. That's the important thing, isn't it?"

"Sure, Jeff," she said. "Of course it is."

sixteen

Our first real argument came when she invited me to a party at Roger Torres' house near the end of April. She actually thought I would be pleased.

"He invited me. He said I should bring you too. He meant it. He wants me to come. He wants us both to come."

"No thanks," I said.

Her face fell twenty miles. "But everybody says he gives the greatest parties. His parents don't bother the kids, and he has this big room at the top of the house where you can see the bridge . . ."

"I know all about it, Ellen. Aren't you forgetting I

used to go to quite a few parties at his house before you came along?"

She was studying me, her face wrinkled in concentration. Thinking came slowly to her. I loved Ellen very much, but I never kidded myself about her mental equipment. Her face brightened.

"If you're worried about Norma . . ."

"I'm not worried about Norma."

"I know that, Jeff. I just mean if you're afraid she'll be upset seeing you, don't worry. She's got a new boyfriend, and she even asked me if I was coming, and if you'd be there."

"Norma has a boyfriend?"

I wasn't jealous. In fact, I was happy she had a boyfriend. I knew I had mistreated her, that she hadn't deserved it, and that I'd hurt her. So, if anything, the news pleased me, even though it was hard thinking of Norma with a boyfriend, like thinking of her with short red hair or wearing a miniskirt.

"Uh huh—a boy named John Kingman."

"Who?"

"John Kingman. He's not in the ceramics class. He doesn't have anything to do with pots. He's in her French class."

"Is he a tall guy with dark hair—wears a gray sweater?"

"No, he's short, sort of ordinary looking—not like you. I think he's supposed to be some kind of math whiz. But he's real nice—everybody likes him."

It embarrassed me how Ellen seemed to follow in the wake of Roger, Dolores, and Norma. How she was fascinated by all their comings and goings, and how she courted their favor and was grateful for any scraps of attention they threw her.

"Norma says he doesn't know a pot from a chandelier, but he hangs around the class a lot, waiting for her. Yesterday, he talked to me about his dog while she was busy unloading the kiln. He has a Doberman pinscher with one blind eye . . ."

"I'm not going to the party, Ellen."

"But why not, Jeff?"

"Because I don't have anything in common with those people anymore."

"But Jeff, I like them."

"Well, why don't you go then? You go by yourself."

Ellen said quickly, "We never go to parties. I like parties."

"Well, why don't you go then? Go right ahead."

"You never want to go anywhere with other people.

You didn't like Nancy and her boyfriend, and you won't ever go to any of the Weight Watchers' parties."

"You can go. I keep telling you—go yourself."

"But you don't mean it, Jeff. You say it, but you don't mean it. You used to go to parties. I know you did. How come you never go anymore?"

"Because I just like to be with you. That's why. Because I'm happiest of all being with you. I don't need any other people."

I was walking her home from school that day. She had lost nearly fifty pounds by then and the rolls of fat on her neck had just about disappeared.

"I think you're ashamed of me," she said. "That's why you don't take me anywhere."

"Are you crazy!" I said to her. "I just love you so much I don't want to share you."

She kept her head down, refusing to look at me. "When you were going around with Norma, you went to parties. You told me you did. And you took her over to your father's house. You never took me to your father's house."

"I took you over to meet my mother."

"Only once. I know she didn't like me. Maybe that's

why you didn't take me to your father's. You're ashamed of me, and you don't want anybody to see us together."

"Ellen, you've got it all wrong. We go out for dinner lots of times, and we meet people and we go to the movies sometimes, and didn't I take you to a couple of basketball games?"

"But most of the time, we stay at my house and just talk. You never really take me anyplace." Her green eyes were angry. "You're ashamed of me," she cried. "I'm trying, but I can't lose weight any faster, and you're ashamed of me."

I grabbed her by the arm and shook her a little.

"Shut up, Ellen, and listen. I'm not ashamed of you. As a matter of fact, I'm satisfied with you just the way you are. I don't even want you to lose any more weight. Why don't you stop right now? It's enough. You look great to me, and I guess all that dieting is making you cranky."

Her eyes opened wide.

"If you want to meet my father, that's fine with me. I warn you, you'll be bored out of your skin, but that's up to you. And if you want to go to parties, okay, we can work that out too. I've got plenty of friends who give parties, if that's what you want. I thought you were happy being with me."

Now she was looking at me again with that familiar, adoring look.

"Oh, Jeff, you know I'm happy with you."

"I thought you were, Ellen, but it doesn't sound as if I was right."

"Oh Jeff, don't say that."

"I didn't say anything. You did."

"Please, Jeff, don't be angry. I'm sorry, Jeff. I'm really sorry."

We didn't go to Roger Torres' party, but I did take her over to my father's house. I know they were surprised by Ellen—especially Wanda. During the evening, she managed to corner me in the kitchen.

"How come, Jeff?" she asked.

"What do you mean?"

"Well, I mean, she's a nice girl, I guess, but Jeff, Norma was gorgeous."

"I think Ellen is gorgeous."

"Okay, okay, don't get sore. Even though she's fat, she isn't bad looking, and her complexion is lovely, but she's . . . well . . ."

"Well what?"

"Well, Norma really has a personality. Ellen just sits there and looks at you."

"You know what, Wanda?"

"What?"

"Mind your own business."

In May, all Ellen could think of was the prom. She ate hardly anything, but even so, she was not going to be losing the eighty pounds she had aimed for. I wanted her to stop dieting altogether. If she had started gaining weight again, I think I would have been happy. Maybe I had begun to realize that with each pound she lost, I was losing something too.

"I'm still going to be fat," she moaned. "And I wanted to be slim."

"Forget it," I told her. "You look great to me, I don't want you to be any thinner. And when you're wearing that gold caftan, you'll look magnificent."

I had called Lady Bountiful in April to ask about the gold caftan for Ellen. They still had some in stock and promised to hold one for us. In the middle of May, I brought Ellen over to the store to try it on. When she emerged from the fitting room, even the saleswoman sucked in her breath.

"You look splendid," she said.

Ellen gleamed like a golden goddess. The caftan flowed around her and her strong neck rose up out of its folds like a column. Her hair was too long and bushy now—she needed a new permanent—but her round, full face with its large green eyes and bright makeup was spectacular. Nobody at that prom would look like my Ellen.

The saleswoman and I discussed accessories and jewelry while Ellen remained motionless in front of the mirror.

"High heels, of course," said the saleswoman. "What do you think of sandals?"

"What color?"

"Oh gold, of course."

"How about jewelry?"

"She has large, gold hoops, but maybe she needs something a little more glamorous."

"Here, let me show you these large, hanging ones with tiny, flashing mirrors. I think they'd be perfect."

"Hmm. Here, Ellen, try these on."

"Jeff," she said. "I'm not sure this dress is right."

"It's magnificent," I told her. "You look like somebody from another world. You're one of a kind in that dress, believe me."

"But don't you think I should go to a regular store and see what they have?"

"No," I said. "This is the dress for you."

She didn't argue. She could have if she didn't agree with me, but she didn't. She took the dress home and even bought the earrings too. I told her she needed a new permanent and she said she would go the day before the prom.

"And I don't want you to see me until you come to pick me up."

"But I thought I'd help you put your makeup on."

"No, no, I can do it myself."

"Well, all right, but don't forget. I want you to use the Babbling Wine lipstick and the violet eye shadow. I think you'd better use a black mascara and go heavy on the eyeliner."

"Sure, Jeff," she said. "Sure."

My father dropped by the hardware store on Wednesday afternoon. The prom was on Saturday. He asked me if I was going to rent a tux, and what my plans were for the night.

"We'll go to dinner first. Mom is lending me the car and I made reservations at Ondine's in Sausalito. Then we'll go to the prom at the Hyatt. I'm not sure what we'll do after."

"That's nice, Jeff," said my father. "The important thing is to have a good time."

"I'll try, Dad."

"Ellen seems like a nice girl."

"Thanks, Dad."

I was waiting for him to leave. But he stood around, looking at me, thinking. "I remember when I went to my prom," he said smiling.

I smiled politely.

"Back in '58. I'll never forget it. Things sure were different then. You didn't go out to dinner, and most of us didn't even have cars."

"Oh?"

"But we always bought flowers for the girls. Are you buying flowers for Ellen?"

"Sure, Dad. That's still the same."

"We used to get roses or maybe an orchid—one of those small ones. The others were too expensive."

"Is that so, Dad?"

My father was grinning to himself. "I didn't have a car. And Marcia's father—the girl I went with, her name was Marcia Berman, nice girl. She became a teacher and married a fellow named Howard Koppel. But anyway, her father was very strict. So he wouldn't lend me his car. He wanted to drive us and pick us up, but I wasn't going to stand for that. Neither was Marcia. She had a lot of spunk. So my friend, Bob Kendall—you remember him, Jeff—a big fellow with a real great sense of humor—well, maybe you don't—you were just a little kid when he moved back East. Well, anyway . . ."

I pretended to be interested in what he had to say, and when he finished, he patted me on the shoulder and said, "I just hope you have as much fun as I did." Then he slipped a bill into my hand. I looked down—it was a one-hundred-dollar bill.

"What's this for?" I said.

"For the prom. I want you to really enjoy yourself. Both of you—I want you to really have a good time."

"But Dad, I saved money for the prom. Really, I have enough."

"It's all right, Jeff. I just want you to have an extra special good time."

On Saturday, my mother was all excited too. Especially when she saw me dressed in the white tux.

"Jeff, you look like—I don't know, Jeff, but there aren't many movie stars as good-looking as you."

"Cut it out, Mom."

"Here, let me fix your bow tie." My mother was grinning from ear to ear. "Oh, Jeff, you're just gorgeous."

"Stop it, Mom!"

But we were both laughing.

"And what about flowers, Jeff?"

"I'm going to pick them up."

"What kind?"

"A wrist corsage—little golden roses, because she's going to be all in gold, Mom. I picked the dress out—a gold caftan, in a shiny, metallic fabric, and big, glittery earrings with little shiny mirrors."

"Mmm!" said my mother, smiling at me. "She'll certainly be proud of you. But here, Jeff, I want to help make the evening a success." She held out a hundred-dollar bill.

"No, Mom, I don't need it. Really, I have plenty of money."

I couldn't tell her that Dad had also handed me a hundred-dollar bill. I didn't want to spoil her good time.

"Go on, Jeff, take it. It'll make me feel like I have a share in tonight's fun. Take it, Jeff, take it."

I caught a glimpse of myself in the hall mirror as I was leaving the house. My mother was right—I looked fantastic. There weren't going to be many guys there tonight looking like me.

I had vacuumed the inside of the car earlier in the evening, and washed and waxed the outside. It gleamed bone clean. I picked up the flowers, honey-colored little roses laced with glittering, golden ribbon for my Ellen's wrist. I watched the florist pack it in one of his boxes, and I carried it out carefully, laid it on the front seat of the car, and headed for Ellen's house.

Five and a half months, I thought to myself as I drove. I've been going with Ellen for five and a half months. When I met her she was ready to kill herself. That night she'd be going to the prom in a magnificent, golden gown, and her joy would be written all over her face. Because of me.

seventeen

Ellen's mother opened the door. Her smile was as big as my mother's.

"Jeff, Jeff," she said. "You look—oh Jeff, you look wonderful."

Her father came out of the living room, shook hands with me and made a few man-type jokes. We all walked back into the living room together.

"Ellen's ready, but I'm under orders to keep you here so she can make a grand entrance. And she certainly does look wonderful. I must say."

"I'm sure she does, Mrs. De Luca. I think that dress is a knockout, and it sure suits her."

Mrs. De Luca hurried out of the room and I could hear her calling up to Ellen, "He's here, Ellen. You can come down now."

Mr. De Luca shook his head proudly. "Women!" he said. Then he moved over to where I was sitting, sat down next to me and said quickly, putting his hand into his pocket, "Listen, Jeff, I know this is costing you a fortune, and my wife and I . . ."

"No!" I told him. "Please don't! My father gave me money, and my mother gave me money, and if I get any more, Ellen and I will charter a yacht and go around the world."

He laughed and took his hand out of his pocket. Then I could hear her steps on the stairs, and in my mind I could see her in the gold caftan, my golden Ellen.

Her mother came in first and pretended to blow a trumpet. "Da, da da da dum dum."

And there she was.

I stood up and smiled.

And then I stopped smiling.

Ellen was standing in the room, giggling softly. She was not wearing the golden caftan. Instead, she had on a long, white dress, low cut with thin little sequined straps. The dress fit her closely. She was still fat, but not so fat that you couldn't see her full bust, her small waist and her large, round hips. And her face—her hair—it was all different. It wasn't my Ellen at all. Instead of a curly Afro, she had a new kind of hairdo with straight, short wisps of hair. Her face had hardly any makeup. She wasn't golden. She was just an ordinary fat girl—maybe a pretty, fat girl but not a golden goddess, not anything to do with me.

"But—why?" I said.

Ellen continued giggling. "I wanted to surprise you," she said. "I didn't want to wear that silly old caftan. I don't have to anymore. I can wear regular sizes now. So I just pretended to buy it. And the earrings too. And then I brought them back, and Mom and I went shopping on Monday. You were working, so you weren't suspicious. And this was the first dress I tried on. See, Jeff, it's a fifteen. I could have taken the thirteen, but Mom thought it would be too tight across the hips. And then yesterday, I went for a haircut. I'm sick of that silly Afro. Everybody's into a layered look now. And see, Mom and Dad gave me these little diamond studs to wear for earrings."

"You brought the gold caftan back?"

"Uh huh, and Mom . . ."

Here Mrs. De Luca chimed in. "I didn't think it was at all appropriate for a prom. Maybe for a statue, but not for a young girl. And she's really got a nice shape now—another few pounds and she'll really be something."

"And then Dad . . ."

"Well," said Mr. De Luca, "of course I don't know anything about clothes, but I hated all that gook she kept putting on her face. I know, Jeff, it was your idea, and when she was really fat, I think it was a great idea. It took her mind off her problems. But now . . ."

"Yes," continued her mother, "now she certainly doesn't need it. She has a wonderful complexion, and just look at all that natural color in her cheeks!"

They went on and on, admiring their dumpy, ordinary daughter in her silly, ordinary dress, while she continued giggling and blushing and looking at me, as if she expected me to join in the chorus of praise and admiration.

I wanted to throw the flowers in her face. I wanted to smack her fat, pink cheeks, and most of all, I wanted to storm out of that house.

Her father was opening a bottle of champagne. "This is a special night for all of us."

Ricky and Matt trooped into the living room and whistled at their sister.

"Turn around, Ellen, and show them the back."

Ellen twirled around, displaying her big, fleshy, bare back with the two sequined straps crisscrossing it. I hated it.

When I handed her the flowers, she cooed over them and attached them to her wrist.

"Lovely, Jeff, just lovely," said her mother. "They're really exquisite."

Ellen began waving her fat arm in the air. "What do you think, Mom?" she asked. "I knew he was going to get yellow ones." She giggled. "He thought they'd go with the caftan."

"Well, well," her mother said quickly, not looking at me, "Yellow works very well with white."

"You know, Jeff," Ellen said, "I nearly called you to say you should get me pink or red roses, but then I figured you'd be suspicious, and Mom said yellow would be fine and so did Nancy."

"Who?"

"Nancy—Nancy Rosenfeld from Weight Watchers. She came shopping with us too, and then we also went and bought these white pumps and the shawl. Nancy said . . ."

Everybody said. She listened to everybody but me. She knew I wanted her to wear the caftan, but she didn't care.

Her father passed around the champagne and toasted us. "To Jeff and Ellen!" he said.

Ellen giggled.

"For a night to remember," said her mother.

More giggles from Ellen.

I don't remember what Ricky and Matt said, but it went on and on and on. Finally Ellen said, "Well, I guess we should go now." And her mother went off and brought a long, white, lacy shawl. She handed it to me to drape around her shoulders, and I could smell the same kind of cheap perfume that Nancy Somebody liked to wear.

"I don't know if you'll be warm enough," said Ellen's mother. "It's a cool night. Maybe you ought to take a warmer jacket—just to wear in the car."

"Oh no, Mom," Ellen said with a mock pout. "I'll be fine." She went over to each member of her family and kissed him or her. You could see everybody found her bewitching.

It wasn't until we were in the car that I told her what I thought.

"Sneaky!" I said. "It was sneaky and mean to keep fooling me—to make me think you were going to wear the caftan."

"But Jeff, I wanted to surprise you."

"No, you didn't," I told her. "You wanted to trick me. You wanted to make a fool of me."

"I hated that dress," Ellen said.

"Well, why didn't you say so?"

"I tried to, Jeff," she said, "but you wouldn't let me."

"Oh, that's great," I told her. "Now you're blaming me. It's my fault. Well, I think it was a pretty lousy trick, and I felt like a real fool standing there. Everybody knew what a jerk I was. Everybody was in on the secret. Everybody but me."

"But Jeff," Ellen said, "don't you like the way I look?"

I didn't hesitate one second. I told her the truth. "No," I said, "I don't like the way you look at all. You look like anybody on the street. You could have looked like a . . . like a goddess, but now you just look ordinary and boring."

She didn't cry. But she turned away from me and looked out of the window and kept quiet all the way to Ondine's. As we got out of the car, she said in a soft voice, "Look, Jeff, it's too late to change anything now. I'm sorry I hurt your feelings. I guess I thought you'd be pleased that I can wear a regular dress like anybody else. You'll see, it will be a wonderful evening anyway. Why don't we just forget it and have a good time."

She took my arm as we walked into the restaurant, but I couldn't forget it. Not even during dinner. We sat at one of the window tables and watched the sky turn rosy pink, but I couldn't forget.

And yet, under my anger, I didn't want it to end. Maybe the evening was ruined for me. Maybe I wanted to ruin it for her too, but that's all. I didn't want it to end. The next day I wanted to start all over again. And I wanted her as much as ever, even in her silly dress.

But I couldn't help feeling betrayed. I had wanted to bring Ellen to the prom as a goddess in a shimmering, golden caftan. Instead, she was like any of the other giggling, silly girls, only fatter.

Norma was there with her new boyfriend. Norma had shed her jeans and old Indian shirts for the evening. Even her fingernails were clean. Her hair still flowed down her back, and in her long, blue dress, she looked like something out of a fairy tale.

She introduced me to her boyfriend, and when the music started up again, he asked Ellen to dance. I had to offer to dance with Norma, but she said, "Why don't we just stand here and talk awhile, Jeff. It's been a long time."

"Okay," I said foolishly. The whole evening was turning into a real drag. I watched Ellen dancing with

Norma's boyfriend, smiling at him with every one of her teeth showing. Norma watched her too. Then she said, "Ellen's a very nice girl, Jeff."

"Mmm."

"I guess it took me a while to get to know her, because—well, I don't mind saying it now, Jeff—I was jealous."

I began mumbling something, but she stopped me.

"No, forget it, Jeff. I have. Or nearly. I realize now what a good person you are, and how hard it must have been for you. I always knew you were sensitive, but now I know you saw something in Ellen nobody else did. You had to be a special person to do what you did—brave and compassionate, too."

She was embarrassing me. I began shaking my head.

"Let me finish, Jeff. I've wanted to say this to you for a long time. It's not easy for me, but I'll feel better after I say it. I was—I am—sorry to lose you. There aren't many boys like you . . ."

"Oh, come on, Norma."

"Just a little more. I think we had a great time, and I'm glad we did. John is different from you. It's a lot of fun. I'm going to Alfred in the fall, and he'll be going to MIT. I guess we'll go on seeing each other. So life is good for me, too, now. I want you to know that, and I want to tell you—you're a nice guy, Jeff."

Ellen was giggling. You could hear her from where we stood.

"Just listen to her," said Norma smiling. "How happy she is now, thanks to you. And doesn't she look lovely? It's hard to remember that just last Christmas, she . . . she . . ."

"Looked like an elephant?" Now I was smiling too.

"She really is very pretty—lovely skin and wonderful green eyes."

"Hmm."

"And so good-natured. And helpful too. Everybody likes her in the ceramics class."

"But she's no good, is she?" I asked.

"What do you mean?" Norma looked puzzled.

"I mean as a potter. She's no good, is she?"

"Well, she's just beginning, so . . ."

"But she'll never be any good, will she?"

"I don't know," Norma said quickly. "You can never tell. She might develop her own special style."

"If you like fat, clumsy, pink pots," I said. "You don't have to pretend, Norma. I won't be insulted."

"Well," Norma said carefully, "she may never become a professional potter, but as long as she enjoys herself, why not?"

The evening dragged along. Ellen talked to everybody. And laughed. Suddenly, it seemed she knew lots of people, and they knew her. She kept squeezing my arm, laughing, talking, pointing out this one and that.

"Look! Look! There's Dolores Kabotie and Roger Torres. Look! They're dancing. No, they're talking to somebody. Oh, look, Jeff! They see me. They're waving. Oh, see, Jeff, they're coming this way."

After the prom, some of the kids had private parties—a couple in the hotel, some at their homes. Ellen wanted to go to all of them. I didn't argue. I went everywhere she wanted. She wasn't thinking of me at all. I was quiet, but I went.

We had breakfast at Cliff House, overlooking the beach, with a bunch of kids I hardly knew. Then all of us greeted the dawn, shivering together down on the damp sand. Somebody made a fire. Ellen borrowed a blanket and draped it around her. A bunch of kids started dancing on the beach, barefoot, still in their evening clothes. Ellen and I sat silently near the fire.

"Look at the sky, Jeff," Ellen said. "I've never seen dawn come up like this. It's so beautiful."

"Hmm!" I said. "I'm cold."

"Here, Jeff, come under the blanket with me. I'm nice and warm."

"I'd like to go home," I told her.

"It's been a wonderful evening," she said. "I'll never forget it."

"That's nice," I said.

Then suddenly everything changed. She turned toward me, and her face was angry.

"Cut it out, Jeff," she said. "Enough's enough."

"What do you mean?"

"You know what I mean. You've been trying to spoil it for me all night. From the moment you saw me in this dress, you tried to spoil it."

"No danger!" I said to her. "You said yourself you had a wonderful time."

"In spite of you," she said. "I did have a wonderful time. But you didn't have anything to do with it. You were too busy being sore. But I can enjoy myself without you."

Her hair lay limp and shapeless on her head, and her face was pale. She had the old gray blanket wrapped around her, covering the silly white dress. I should have stopped myself. I should have said, "Okay, Ellen, let's drop it." But I didn't. Maybe everything would have been all right if I had. Maybe not.

"And you can make a fool of yourself too," I told her, "without me. Playing up to everybody—especially that ceramics crowd. They just throw you a couple of bones because they're sorry for you . . ."

"No," said Ellen, her green eyes very bright and fierce. "No. They like me. They . . ."

"They're sorry for you."

"Norma really likes me. She gave me one of her pots. She . . ."

"She said you'll never be a good potter. That's what she said. Everybody knows that except you. You keep wasting your time making ugly pots, but you just don't have the knack and you never will."

Ellen jumped up and tore off the blanket. The morning winds blew her white dress around her and whipped up her hair into spikey points. She screamed at me in a loud voice, so loud that a bunch of the kids who were dancing on the beach stopped and stared at us.

"I hate you, Jeff!" she screamed. "I hate you! I hate you!"

eighteen

It was all over after that night. For a while, I kept calling and calling. I talked to her mother and her father and even her brothers. They all thought she had gone crazy.

But she said no. And she stayed angry. When I talked to her, I could hear the anger in her voice sizzling over the phone.

"I said I was sorry," I told her. "Okay, so I was a jerk. It's all over now. I was wrong and I'm sorry."

"No," she said fiercely. "You belittle me. You always belittle me."

"Belittle?" I said. "What kind of a word is that—*belittle*?"

"There!" she cried. "You're doing it again. You'll always do it with me. You think you own me. You think I can't do anything by myself or think anything by myself or say anything."

"Okay," I said, "so go ahead and say *belittle*."

"I'll say anything I like," she said angrily. "I don't need you to tell me what to say."

"I just don't know why you're making such a big fuss. You never were like this before."

"No, because I was your slave before, and I'm not going to be your slave anymore. I'm tired of feeling trapped. All those years I was trapped inside being a fat girl, and then you came along . . ."

"That's right," I said. "I came along and let you out, didn't I?"

"No," she yelled. "You didn't let me out. You locked me up again. It was the power—that's all you ever wanted. You never really loved *me!* But I'm not going to play that game anymore. I'm going to do what I want from now on."

"Fine," I said. "So who's stopping you?"

"That's right," she answered. "Nobody."

The last time I called her was when I received notice from U.C. San Diego that I had been accepted.

"Hi, Ellen, I just heard from San Diego. I've been accepted," I said, trying to sound low-key.

"That's nice," came her sulky voice over the phone.

"How about you? Have you heard anything?"

"Last week. I got in too."

"Well, look, that's great. And Ellen, why don't we get together and talk it over?"

"I'm not going, Jeff. I'm going to stay here and keep taking lessons from Ida O'Neill."

I remained silent.

"I don't care what you think, Jeff. I don't care what anybody thinks. I'm going to learn to be a potter—a good potter. That's what I want to do, and that's what I'm going to do, and nobody's going to talk me out of it. Not you! Not my parents! Not anybody!"

How deluded can anybody get? In a million years, she'd never be a potter. Everybody else knew it. Everybody but Ellen.

And that's how we broke up. Over a delusion. Maybe I had a delusion too. I had saved Ellen, and I guess I thought she could do the same for me. I had created her: She was—she is my handiwork. Everything she is today is because of me—even her delusion about becoming a potter.

I took it hard. The nightmares came back. I wandered around at night and tried to avoid my mother. But she heard. I pretended I was worried about finals, but one night she got it out of me.

I was sitting in the kitchen, eating bananas. But they weren't helping me feel any better.

"What is it, Jeff? What's wrong? This is the fourth night in a row that you've been up," said my mother.

"It's nothing, Mom. I'll be all right. I'm sorry I keep waking you up."

"That's okay, Jeff. You know I never sleep much. But what's wrong? Is something wrong?"

I looked at her tight, little face and I felt exhausted. I was tired of her and tired of her problems. When I had Ellen, I could forget. But now it was there again, and it seemed to me that all my life I'd been worrying about my mother and her problems. I could see ahead to all the years stretching out in front of me, filled with wakefulness, and frightening dreams, and late nights in the kitchen with her and her problems.

"Jeff, you're crying," said my mother. "My poor boy, what is it?"

She put her skinny arms around me and pressed my head against her bony chest. She was rocking me and it made me angry. I pulled away from her and said, "Ellen's left me."

"Ellen?" My mother blinked. "Ellen left you!"

"Ellen left me," I repeated.

"Why, that's crazy," said my mother.

"Why is it crazy?"

"Well, I know you liked her, Jeff, but really, even aside from her weight, I never could understand how you ever could have given up Norma for a girl like Ellen."

"You didn't like Norma when I was going around with her," I snapped. "You always had nasty little things to say about Norma."

"Well, I might have objected to the way she dressed—she certainly was sloppy—but at least she was a nice girl, a pretty girl, and kind of interesting too, I thought. But Ellen . . ."

"That's right," I said. "Ellen can't hold a candle to Norma. She doesn't have a brain in her head, and when I met her nobody could stand her. I was her only friend. If it weren't for me, she'd still be a fat, ugly hulk without a friend in the world." I ranted on and on for a while, and my mother said, "You did a lot for that girl."

"You don't know the half of it," I said. "I taught her how to dress, how to walk, even how to think. I was the one who even got her started in ceramics. And if she'd listen to me, she'd realize that she can't do it. I only want what's best for her, but she won't listen."

"They never do," said my mother, shaking her head. "You give up your whole life for them, and they don't appreciate it. They don't thank you for what you've done. They spit in your face and then they go away and . . ."

She didn't finish the sentence, but I could have finished it for her. They go away and live their lives without you. Like Wanda, like my father, and now like Ellen.

My mother took my hand and pressed it. "My poor boy," she said gently, "you're better off without her. A boy like you won't have any trouble finding somebody else. You'll feel better after a while. You'll get over it."

My poor mother and I were linked in our misery. And in too many other ways. It chilled me as we sat there that night consoling each other. But it helped me too. I wasn't going to end up like her if I could help it. I wasn't going to spend my life brooding over how other people had disappointed me. In the fall, I would be leaving too.

I saw Ellen in school today. We'll be graduating in a few days, and after that, maybe I won't see her again for a long time. She was carrying a pot in her hand, looking at it with joy, the same way Norma had been looking at the pot in her hands the first time I saw her. I don't remember Norma's pot, but it couldn't have looked anything like Ellen's. It couldn't have been squat and lumpy and glazed in a shiny vomit pink. Ellen's face was rosy. She was wearing jeans and an old T-shirt, and she looked like any other pretty, chubby girl.

"Hi, Ellen," I said as she passed.

She looked up. There was still a smile on her lips from her pleasure over the ugly little pot. But when she saw me, her face hardened. She nodded, averted her eyes, and hurried away.

I saw my advisor there too. He shook my hand and congratulated me on getting into U.C. San Diego.

"Well, we got you through, Jeff, didn't we?" he said heartily.

His eyes were already moving around me to the dozen or so people in his office, waiting to see him.

"I just wanted to thank you," I told him, "and also to say I wish I had taken your advice about one thing."

"What was that, Jeff?" he asked.

"I should have taken Mr. Wasserman for chemistry."

About the Author

Marilyn Sachs is the author of more than forty books, including *A Pocket Full of Seeds*, *Lost in America*, and *First Impressions*, and was a National Book Award finalist for *The Bear's House*. She lives in San Francisco.

Afterword

The Fat Girl was originally published in 1984. It was typed on an electric typewriter, which seemed to me at the time, the greatest advancement of technology. Naturally, I was wrong. Today, I type this on a fancy computer, which can sing songs, show photos, and tell me just about anything I want to know about anybody.

So many changes in the last twenty-two years. But not everything changes. Not the misuse of power. That never changes, ever since the beginning of recorded history.

It took me a couple of years to write *The Fat Girl* because I never seemed to get it right. First, I thought I wanted to write a love story about a kind boy who tries to help a fat girl in his class who was dying of leukemia—let's make it a ceramics class—and ends up falling in love with her. They enjoy a perfect romance until she dies. I wrote five or six chapters very happily, and then gave up in disgust. Maybe because I suddenly realized that generations of other writers had already written that story or one very much like it, that it was trite, and, in any case, I was bored with it.

But I didn't want to give it up because there was something in the story that intrigued me. What was it?

Perhaps, I thought, I should write a story about a fat girl who says she's dying. Perhaps she says she's dying so that she can get the attention of a very attractive, popular boy in her class—still the ceramics class—who would otherwise be off limits for her.

So I started all over again, wrote several chapters, and felt I was finally heading in the right direction. But then, one day, I looked at what I had written, and realized, no, this wasn't it either. Still, I had a feeling that there was something there that was eluding me, something that I really wanted to write about.

I made a few more attempts. For a while, the fat girl became a fat boy—but the ceramics class remained. There was something about that ceramics class that was important even though I couldn't quite figure out what it was. Finally, I put the manuscript aside for a few months and tried to work on something else. There have been a number of books in my career that I have had to give up completely, but I didn't want to give up on this one. I kept thinking about it, and then one day I realized what it was that kept plaguing me about *The Fat Girl*, what was buried in the story, why it had to take place in a ceramics class, and what I really wanted to write about. I wanted to write about power.

Most of us know the Greek myth of Pygmalion, the sculptor, who creates a beautiful statue named Galatea, falls in love with her, and through the power of his love, convinces the gods to bring her to life. We are all meant to be on Pygmalion's side, and to believe that the beautiful statue will be so happy at turning into a real live woman that she will adore Pygmalion, and live happily ever after with him. But nobody knows for sure what Galatea really felt.

I thought I knew.

So *The Fat Girl*, as it was finally written, involves a confused boy who attempts to change an unhappy, fat girl into his modern Galatea. Although his intentions, in the beginning, are really kind and generous, his increasing power over her changes him into a dangerous tyrant. I believe this to be true of anyone who has power, whether it be the dictators all over the present world, Pygmalion, or Jeff Lyons in *The Fat Girl*.

—Marilyn Sachs, 2007

Discussion Questions for
The Fat Girl

1. Why is the book called *The Fat Girl*? Is the "fat girl" the protagonist? Why or why not?

2. In his references to "that year" and "what might have been," Jeff indicates that he's telling this story looking back. How old do you think Jeff, the narrator, is? And has he changed at all since his senior year of high school?

3. When Jeff yells at Ellen for breaking his teapot, she is "smiling a kind of pleading, frightened smile that

made me want to punch her." Why does Jeff feel that way? Later he thinks, "I wondered what the fat girl would feel like, and I wanted to puke." Why and when do his feelings change? (See pages 25, 37.)

4. Reread Jeff's conversation with Norma about his fear of the dark. (See page 28.) What is your reaction? Is there anything unsaid?

5. Do you agree with Jeff that he and Norma would have stayed together if it wasn't for Ellen? Why or why not?

6. List all the things Jeff says he feels jealous about. Why do each of these things bother him? Although we use the words *jealous* and *envious* as synonyms sometimes, they are actually slightly different. To be envious is to want something someone has. To be jealous is to fear losing something you have. Is Jeff jealous or envious in each of these situations?

7. "I still hoped she wouldn't take ceramics next term, wouldn't be there watching me, disturbing my balance and, most of all, making me forget that I was a nice guy. Like Norma said, that's what I am, a nice guy." Why does Ellen make Jeff forget he's a nice guy? What does Jeff mean when he says he *forgets* to be a nice guy? Why does it bother him not to be "a nice guy"? What do you think it means to be a "nice person"? (See page 44.)

8. Why did Jeff feel so freaked out about Ellen threatening to kill herself even after her mother said it was an empty threat? Do you think Ellen was serious?

9. Why did Jeff's relationship with Norma end? (See page 127.)

10. Why was Jeff irritated when people were surprised to see him with Ellen? (See page 130.)

11. How are Ellen and Jeff's nighttime fears related? What is Jeff afraid of?

12. Why is it that Jeff says, "I didn't want anyone helping me with Ellen." What are other people trying to do? What is he trying to do? (See page 86.)

13. How does Jeff react to Wanda leaving? Why does he feel he's going to "lose something else that belongs to me"? What else has he lost? (See page 98.)

14. What did you think when you first read Jeff's statement "I knew that I had brought her back from the dead and made a human being of her. She belonged to me now and I would never let her go"? How do you feel about that statement now?

15. Why does Jeff compare Aunt Lisa and Wanda? (See page 156.)

16. What does Jeff mean when he says, "Poor Wanda! I felt sorry for her. Poor Mom! Poor Dad! I was sorry for all of them, because I was safe and very high on Ellen"? (See page 160.)

17. What does Jeff feel he's losing with each pound Ellen loses? (See page 188.)

18. Compare the argument Jeff has with his mom on pages 13-15 and the argument he has with Ellen on pages 143-147. What are the differences in how he narrates each scene?

19. Do you believe Jeff when he says he's not going to end up like his mother? Why or why not? (See page 213.)

20. Marilyn Sachs says this story came from her "fascination with the question of power." When does a helping hand become a stranglehold? When does love turn into a trap? How would you answer those questions in terms of this story or in your experience?

21. Research the myth of Pygmalion or watch *My Fair Lady*, a musical based on the Pygmalion story. What parallels do those stories have with *The Fat Girl?*

22. The story is told from Jeff's perspective. What would be different if it were told by Ellen? What does she have to say that Jeff leaves out? When do we finally hear from her, and what does she have to say?